TED ALLBEURY

A Choice of Enemies

PANTHER
Granada Publishing

Panther Books
Granada Publishing Ltd
8 Grafton Street, London W1X 3LA

Published by Panther Books 1976
Reprinted 1976, 1979, 1982, 1983, 1985

First published in Great Britain by
Peter Davies Ltd 1973

Copyright © Ted Allbeury 1973

ISBN 0-583-12493-3

Printed and bound in Great Britain by
Collins, Glasgow

Set in Times

'*A man cannot be too careful in the choice of his enemies.*'

OSCAR WILDE

Author's Note

In writing about the British Army in
Germany in 1944 it would be pointless to
avoid using the correct names of such large
commands as 21 Army Group and 30 Corps,
but I wish to emphasize that names of units
and persons are all fictitious.

CHAPTER ONE

The map on the wall said 'Land Braunschweig and Regierungsbezirk Hildesheim – nur für Militärgebrauch'. This was the area my units covered and alongside was a street map of my headquarters town – Hildesheim itself. Useless, of course, as the lovely fifteenth-century buildings had been eighty per cent flattened by the U.S. 5th Air Force in a little under seven minutes. The heaps of rubble had erased the pattern of the streets but the remaining buildings had had paths beaten to them, and round them, by a flow of military vehicles. Our own target for tonight was what used to be 52 Hohensen and was one of the few usable blocks of flats.

It was June '45 and my Field Security Section was in its third month of round-the-clock arrests of the usual mixed bag of Gestapo, Abwehr, SS and other odd bodies. Most days there was a 'special' – so designated by 21 Army Group. 'Specials' were generally picked up in the middle of the night as it was reckoned that the sudden rousing from sleep and immediate interrogation was likely to produce quicker results than a daytime arrest. Group were dead right, of course, but it did leave an odd period after dinner from about nine to midnight when you were sitting around tensed up while the rest of the world, civil and military, was settling itself down for the night.

The NCOs passed the time playing cards or listening to several hundred Vivaldi concerti, according to taste. I always sat around in my own quarters, a lavish suite on the first floor. In the early days I used to gaze vacantly over the town, but we soon rumbled that it was a dead give-away that there was going to be a raid that night, and now the curtains were drawn and a fire burned bright, but it wasn't a bit like home. A superb Bechstein concert grand suffered my version of 'My very good friend the milkman' and offering no encouragement to further exploration, I was left to

7

my own devices. A kind of ritual spread itself over this waiting time. Too tense to read, I generally sipped a whisky with all the phoney relish of a non-drinker trying to feel as other men are. After four years of tracking down and arresting Italians and Germans, of one shade of naughtiness or another, with gusto and no second thoughts, I knew that I was suffering the occupational hazard of identifying with the other guy. Doing it all in peacetime seemed more difficult than it should.

The object of 21 Army Group's affection tonight was a Luftwaffe colonel. According to the records, he had given, or passed, the order for several recaptured RAF officers to be shot. We had kept tabs on him for several days. He looked, as usual, more like a tired grey-haired bank manager than a Luftwaffe colonel. He had a wife and daughter and a son in a Panzer division that got clobbered near Falaise.

I found I was having the same crazy thoughts that had started up a week or two ago. There ought to be some way of warning 'specials' to use their evening well. More than likely he was reading some book not worth reading or quarrelling with his wife. Using up the last few hours of freedom in some ridiculous ordinary human way. And I sat around doing the same. I could hear Jacko running my car engine and then revving up the light truck to get it warm. A knock, and the sergeant-major came in grinning and holding out my web belt, newly green blanco'd complete with Smith & Wesson.

'Signal just come in from 21 AG, sir – suspect may be armed.'

'Wonder who the source was.'

'Didn't indicate, sir – just keeping us on our toes more likely. I rang 5 Division and laid on light for one-thirty, sir.'

All power and lighting was cut off at the power station at 11 p.m., except for the military circuits, and the army engineers generally laid on lighting for any buildings we were raiding. It impressed the local gentry and made things easier for us. We sometimes called on the real military for a few bodies to 'stake out' a building, but our little lot had pleaded unit celebrations tonight. In fact, the liars were off on their own private sport. Way back I had made the mistake of giving their platoon commanders a lecture on military co-operation with intelligence units, and had cited the case of Martín Bormann with much detail and photographs. They now carried out Bormann exercises deploying hundreds of troops twice a week, and with such enthusiasm and rivalry that I had not yet found the courage to tell them that he had been positively indentified in Caracas in early June. It kept them happy and in what the General called 'a mood of alert aggression'. It did a lot too to save the lads from stretches in the glass-house as it was part of the long, grey period when the conquerors were hot against fraternization – for troops anyway – till Military Government had had first pick.

There was a good moon, but the glare of the headlights and the noise of the vehicles sounded absolutely indecent in the quiet still of the night. The block of flats concerned was more-or-less intact and the outside door was closed and locked. We had all done lock-picking courses with the Portsmouth police, but the sergeant-major was the only one who remembered how to do it. Rumour had it that he knew all about it long before we were sent down to Portsmouth. I think I was the only one who had faith in his innocence, apart from our recruiting branch who also knew that, in fact, he had specialized in drug and gun-running in his formative pre-1939 years.

With not much fiddling the door groaned open and right on the nail the lights went on. The next bit was mine; protocol and the niceties had vaguely got together so that the actual arrest was always done by me. I seemed to have spent a lifetime walking up the stairways of flats in the middle of the night. There was a marked difference between the performance in Italy and Germany. In Italy neither party took the matter in hand too seriously; it was all too obviously a mistake. But in Germany it was all very real. No movement as you traipsed up the stairs, but a miasma of cabbage and fear. You felt you were actually doing what

9

you were doing – in earnest. The way they did it themselves. Maybe it was all this stuff about the Royal Family still ruling Hanover. Maybe they still weren't used to the idea that it could happen to them.

There was no light on inside flat 17, so I gave the bell a good long jab and flipped up the button on my holster. The usual scufflings went on inside, and with much unlocking and unchaining, the colonel half opened the door.

'Herr Lemke.' The mister reassured him; it always did.

'Ja.'

'Oberst-Leutnant Lemke.'

The colonel bit dug home and he suddenly looked about ninety. Inside the hall we went through all the ritual dance of what it was all about. I agreed that I was sure he had always been correct and confirmed that it might have to do with the RAF officers at Poznan. He tried me out on how misguided they were, trying to escape again after recapture, and I played it back that we had two eye-witnesses to say that two were shot in the back peeing in a hedge while handcuffed, and the general chat sort of died. A long harangue by the lady colonel on democracy and British justice and at long last we had collected blanket and razor and that was that. Lady colonel asked when we would be back and the answer did no good for British justice. The colonel's daughter, both in and out of a nightie, eyed me speculatively and, I felt, was considering some sort of swop for Dad and finally came down on the side of reporting me to her friend the Military Governor. I booked Lemke in the jail and decided he wouldn't be difficult and left the interrogation till the morning. Jacko was waiting up for me like a real mother with hot milk and news of a Leica for five hundred Woodbines. I asked about the cat, who had apparently not yet had her kittens, and had disappeared early in the afternoon. The thought of bed was so good and I noticed it was clean sheet day. I really was tired and it was bliss to stretch my legs down the bed.

Nothing in my extensive training prepared me for the feel of my bare feet coming to rest on a tired cat and nine damp kittens.

CHAPTER TWO

Jacko and tea. And three messages on my signal pad. I wondered what VJ day was, but whatever it was, 21 AG was concerned that I should know today was it. Two SS men we picked up three weeks ago had escaped and laid out a major in the Military Police as they went, and my help would be appreciated. Finally, the new Deputy Director of Military Intelligence had reached the decision that webbing would be scrubbed and not blanco'd.

'And Major Howe's been on the blower several times already, sir.'

'O.K., Jacko, buzz him for me now.'

Major Howe of Military Government had his diplomatic voice on, thick with insincerity.

'Alors, tout va bien, mon Commandant.'

'Cut it out, George – what are you after?'

'Nothing me boy – nothing at all. I just thought you'd like to know I've got four brand new tyres for a Merc and they're all yours.'

'For what?'

'For nothing – just appreciation.'

'What appreciation?'

'You know – justice, co-operation and all that.'

The word 'justice' rang all the bells and I knew where we were. 'You mean the Military Governor isn't getting justice and co-operation from his girl friend.'

'Well, I wouldn't put it like that exactly.'

'How would you put it, George?'

'Look – do it for me, pal.'

'No.'

'Well, come round now and just have a drink.'

'I don't drink.'

'What – not even tea?'

'Fair enough, George – in twenty minutes.'

Major Howe and I had sweated through a parachute

course together and he was old enough to be my father and a bit to spare. He was now put out to graze in the quietness of Military Government. On his desk was a photograph of a lovely blonde woman set in a silver frame. This was George's wife. She had left him years ago, but he got some sort of crazy satisfaction out of weaving a romantic fantasy round this woman and I was one of the few who had claims on his affection by saying the right word from time to time. Tea was being served in Meissen china and I remarked on this ladylike touch.

'It was "beschlagnahmt" for me personally by the Burgermeister.'

'Did he get those tyres as well?'

He looked up and seemed more serious than I had expected. 'Forget the tyres old lad and the Military Governor for a minute.'

'Hope my lot haven't bugged your office or we'll both be on the mat.'

'You're two men short right now, aren't you?'

'Three at the end of the month.'

'How'd you like a fully trained, experienced man – four languages, the lot?'

'How'd the Military Governor like a nice blonde with full security clearance?'

'I thought we'd be able to talk.'

We got down to the white-slaving and I made out a clearance for a Fräulein Lemke and skipped over the bits that hurt. My lucky draw was an American CIC sergeant who had opted for his release in Germany and was looking for a job. I set up an interview for that afternoon.

* * *

You would have had to have some years in counter-intelligence to appreciate the man who marched into my office that afternoon. They say Isaac Stern is a violinist's violinist; and Louis Berger was a spy-catcher's spy-catcher. He was short, with a craggy red face and looked tough as old boots. He was a shade older than me – say thirty – and his eyes took in the room as if he might have to fight his way

12

out. He wore his sergeant's uniform as if he hated it. He didn't sit till I asked him to.

He had opted for demob from U.S. counter-intelligence in Germany and had approached Major Howe to get alongside me. He had the languages and the training. He showed me two volumes of the Milice reference book in which there was an 'M' against his name as wanted dead or alive, and that was good enough for me.

There was a German underground movement down in the south of my area at Alfeld and I briefed him and arranged for him to start on the job in two days' time.

After about ten days, there were signs that Berger was moving around. Complaints from the German police and local populace – the usual stuff. Berger had set up a furniture shop as his cover and wasn't being too fussy where the stock came from. Neither was I. We didn't have enough funds to be that fussy.

Like most people on intelligence work, I had a strong streak of feminine intuition – bells would ring and then I'd start looking round for what didn't fit. I was stretched out in the bath when the bells rang this time and it was something to do with Milice handbooks. I came out of the bath with a rush like the sea-lions at feeding time. The 'M' wasn't for 'morte' it was for 'Mord' – murder. The Milice didn't use capitals, but the Kripo handbook did. He'd shown me the cover of one and the opened pages of the other.

I was in Alfeld within the hour and checked with my detachment the location of Berger's shop. He'd also taken a house and on a Sunday afternoon, I guesed that's where he would be. I went in through the kitchen window; there was no one on the ground floor and I moved upstairs. One bedroom door was closed and I guessed that would be it. I pointed the Smith & Wesson sideways and put my foot on the door. The lock held – then sprang – and the door flew open. Berger was only half awake, in bed with a girl. We were both professionals and he must have known that it was more or less over. I had to listen to ten minutes of righteous indignation on how he was just building up an

13

operations fund. It was worth the ten minutes because I didn't know why he was wanted for murder and his reactions to what I had to say might give a clue to the set-up. He had worked for CIC all right because I'd checked. But I had a strong feeling that he wasn't an American, and if he was on the Kripo books for murder, the odds were that he was an old boy from the Gestapo training school in Berlin. Probably done a little job on his own account and then laid low until the Americans came. The accent was New York or Chicago – I didn't know enough to place it exactly – and then he got to the bit where we would share out the seven thousand quid between us and call it a day.

I felt almost sorry for him – it's not easy making a pitch looking down the wrong end of a gun and it's well nigh impossible when you haven't got your trousers on and the other guy's wearing a uniform. And then he was finished. I let him roast in silence for a bit. 'That's not what I want you for, Berger.' He didn't bat an eye, but he did close his mouth. The first line of natural defence that the real pro takes. I waited for him to ask what I did want him for, but he was silent – like a trap ready to spring. I had a small problem. Too much hurry and too little organization. I was on my own and the phone was down by the front door. The solution was embarrassing for all concerned. Embarrassing for them because I made them go downstairs as they were – stark naked – and with the front door open, they stood on the steps outside. There was plenty of sunshine and we drew quite a crowd.

Embarrassing for me because although he looked as red and raw as a badly plucked turkey, Berger knew that he was doing his Adam and Eve act in public because I'd boobed. I used one hand on the phone to get my local boys round. Berger and the redhead went in the back of the truck and one of the sergeants gave them a mixed bag of their clothes after checking them for contents.

'Take them up to Hildesheim, Sergeant – in the town nick – our bit, and separate cells. Don't let them talk on the way.'

'Right, sir.'

'Where's Lieutenant Boyle?'

'Up in the bedroom, sir.'

I called upstairs as I went and Blair Boyle's big grin took the tension away.

'Blair, I want you to go over the whole place. Every bit of paper to the Document Unit – check all local bank accounts that have increased in the last two weeks and check the garden. Get any bods you want from 5 Div but give MilGov a miss till I tell you.'

'Can you give me any idea what we're looking for?'

'No, I haven't a clue.'

I got back to Hildesheim from Alfeld late, about eleven, and there was a note to ring George Howe and a galley proof of tomorrow's *Hannoversche Kurier* with a dirty great headline. Just one word – a long German word – it said 'SIPPENBESTRAFUNG'. In English, it's even longer, because it means 'visiting the sins of the fathers on their sons'. In this case, for sons, you read daughters. The story covered my arrest of Colonel Lemke for 'an alleged crime in the heat of war' and went on to say how, out of revenge, I had ordered his daughter to be dismissed from her post as secretary to the Military Governor without even checking on her background. The writer understood that a complaint was to be lodged with the Control Commission, etc., etc., and there was a good picture of the colonel's daughter, looking very blonde and very pretty, wearing white cotton stockings.

I phoned George Howe who sounded distinctly wary: 'Have you seen tomorrow's paper, old boy?'

'Don't old boy me, you bastard – what's the big idea.'

'The MilGov's got the wind up – given her the push.'

'What about the security clearance I gave you?'

'There's a question down in the House next week about the RAF officers and the old boy's had second thoughts – so if it's O.K. by you, I'll dispose of the clearance and we'll all go back to square one.'

'And I'm left holding the baby – English Gestapo and all that crap.'

'You know you don't give a damn.'

15

'I guess you're right – but I'll have to rake her in for a check now – just for the record.'

'She's not a bad kid.'

I didn't follow it up because to Major Howe, DSO, every blonde in the world was the one in the silver frame. I had no idea how he felt about redheads, but I didn't mention that his peace offering, Berger, was just about settling down for the night in George's own nick.

Jacko came in with a cup of china tea. I'd never had the heart to tell him that I loathed the stuff, so I sat sipping it infrequently while we talked about the progress of the kittens. They now lived happily in a large cardboard box at the side of my bed. I gathered that Jacko felt that such a touch of domesticity right in my own bedroom would keep me on the straight and narrow. George Howe had once heard Jacko beating round this particular bush and had pointed out that I wasn't even married and Jacko came out fighting and declared, 'The captain isn't interested in that sort of thing, sir!' George didn't look impressed.

There was a message beside my bed that Martin Bormann had just slipped through the hands of a 5 Div raiding party, but they were hot on the trail and would keep me informed. I was too tired to care even if it had been true. I looked at my pack of antaphrodisiac cats and switched out the light.

CHAPTER THREE

Next morning it was clear that the *Hannoversche Kurier* had done its job well, but arse about face. Injustice may have been exposed, but the pile of messages showed that the locals had not survived the Weimar Republic and the Third Reich without being nippy on their feet. If the English Gestapo could put it over on the MilGov, then they could be counted on to find jobs and rations, help wives jail husbands, annul marriages and give the Lutheran Bishop priority for his church windows. The Prussian colonels had met their match and the boys were in there pitching for me. There was a cool sort of signal from 21 AG via 30 Corps via the DDMI. 'To CI officer Hildesheim stop Send full details Lemke affair to Judge Advocate's dept 21 AG stop.'

I didn't get around to Fräulein Lemke for about three days. The interrogation report on her father was on my desk. He had passed on the order from the OKW and had made no protest of any kind; he was already in a full interrogation camp in North Wales. The Lemke girl had been given a Fragebogen to fill in and she wasn't a member of anything. I looked at it carefully and then gave her a good long look.

'Have you got anything to add, Fräulein Lemke?'

'My father didn't kill those RAF officers – he couldn't do such a thing.'

'True enough, Miss Lemke – he just passed the order on to somebody else.'

'An order is an order.'

'Well, we're here to talk about you right now. I see you were not a member of any party organization.'

'That's right.'

'What kind of stockings are you wearing?'

'Nylons,' and then she suddenly realized the point of the question and she knew she had been exposed in her phoney piece of defiance.

17

'Miss Lemke, when you posed for the newspaper photograph, you wore white cotton stockings which are part of the uniform of the BDM – you knew that all the German readers would get the point and you thought we wouldn't. Were you a member of the BDM?'

'No, never.'

'Why did you wear the stockings then?'

'I was angry about my father and losing my job and when it was suggested it seemed a good idea.'

'Who did the suggesting?'

She hesitated, bit her lip and finally said, 'The reporter.'

That would come in very handy. She was clean as a whistle politically; in fact, she must have had quite a tough time just because she didn't join anything.

'I'm sorry you lost your job – I'll fix you up with another.'

I phoned Personnel at MilGov, but they weren't going to touch her with a barge-pole. I tried the Arbeitsamt but the word had gone out there too. All they could offer was what they called 'rehabilitation' work which meant shifting bomb damage rubble and she didn't deserve that, even if her old man was Colonel Lemke.

I rang the British Army Liaison Officer at the *Hannoversche Kurier*, but they were quite happy to let justice take a beating if it depended on them. I shoved the phone aside and looked at Fräulein Lemke.

'How much did you get at MilGov?'

'Two hundred marks a month.' The General had obviously had a very good buy.

'Fair enough – well, you'll start here tomorrow in charge of the German household staff – same pay as MilGov and we'll clear you with the Arbeitsamt.'

CHAPTER FOUR

During the next few days I had long talks with Berger, there was no point in making it a formal interrogation. He was in the business and he was clammed up tight about anything further back than when he joined me. The American CIC records were pretty scanty and he had an address in New York that didn't exist so there was not much to go on there. The record said he was highly efficient and his work had led to the arrest of some quite naughty boys.

Berger wanted to know what he would get. I suggested it would be four to nine months and this seemed to set him back a lot. On the last days before he was to be tried he was desperate to do a deal and at the final talk he offered £5,000 cash paid into a Swiss account if I'd call it off. There was something out of proportion in the set-up; it didn't worry me but it didn't make sense.

After all, he was going to be done on civil charges, as it didn't seem worth while trying to establish the evidence of how he had conned the CIC and George Howe – not to mention your humble servant – and if he'd murdered anyone it was surely a German, and we could hardly hold that against him. But Berger seemed to be fencing around like his life depended on it. Anyway, I'd got enough to fix him in the civil court, and when I got up to leave, he offered me the money, his mistress and his very nice Buick sedan. In fact, his money was with the Judge Advocate's department, the Quartermaster-Sergeant had his name down for the mistress, and Jacko was checking over the Buick for me.

It didn't seem a very difficult case, so I acted as prosecuting officer myself. Berger refused to testify, and refused to answer all questions despite a threat of contempt of court, but the evidence of theft and extortion was easy to establish. There was no jury and a Military Government Judge was summing up and it was quite clear that Berger was going to be found guilty. '... and in view of the fact that the accused not only carried out these unlawful acts, but claimed or purported to be a member of HM Forces, in order to bring pressure to bear on his victims, this Court finds the defendant guilty, and sentences him to six months' imprisonment. Louis Alexander Berger, have you anything that you wish to say to this Court?'

Berger looked very pale, stood up, and looking at me not the Judge, said: 'This Court has no power to try me. I am not a German citizen.' The colonel who was acting as Judge looked over the top of his glasses, shuffled through his papers and pulled one to one side, and took several minutes to read it. 'Mr Berger, you have not been tried as a German citizen but as an American citizen, demobilized from the United States Army. You were demobilized in Germany at your own request, and I have here a document from the United States Consul, at Hamburg, authorizing any Court in the jurisdiction of the British Military Government to bring you to trial with the status of a U.S. citizen voluntarily resident in the British Occupied Zone of Germany. You were offered the services of an officer from the Judge Advocate's department of the United States Army, as entitled by the Veterans Administration Act. You were also offered the services of a German civilian lawyer. In both cases you refused these offers – unwisely in my opinion – and the sentence passed upon you by this Court will stand.' And the colonel patted his papers into neat piles, and I bent down to do the same with mine. And the few people in the Court relaxed, and communally we sucked our teeth with the feeling that, if not well done, the job was at least done.

'I am a Belgian citizen, and this Court has no power to try me.'

There was complete silence and slowly the colonel said: 'You are claiming Belgian citizenship, Mr Berger?'

'Yes.'

'Where were you born, Mr Berger?'

'Bruges.'

'Well, Mr Berger, if this is the case, you have wasted the Court's time in not making your position clear before these proceedings started.' Without waiting for a reply from Berger, the Judge turned to me and said, 'Well, Captain Bailey, what have you in mind?'

My legal knowledge was very thin and certainly only good enough to carry me through an open and shut case, but I'd read enough last chapters of detective stories to know what the ploy was – when in doubt ask for an adjournment.

'Sir, I should like to ask the Court for an adjournment, so that certain inquiries can be made.'

'Of course, and what period of time are you suggesting the Court should give you?'

'Twenty-one days, sir.' This caused two very raised eyebrows and a rather quizzical look.

'Oh no, Captain – oh no. This Court will adjourn for seven days to allow further inquiries to be made.'

I put a call through to the Judge Advocate's department at 21 AG, and they agreed to send me down as officer next day. But next day my visitors were David Law, a Military Intelligence liaison officer, and a Lieutenant Lemaire of the Belgian Sureté. We made ourselves comfortable and I doled out whiskies all round.

David Law raised his glass and with a broad grin said, 'Well, my boy, looks like you've been conned twice over.'

'Yep – time spent in reconnaissance is seldom wasted and all that.'

'Well, fill us in and we'll see if we can sort it out for you.'

I gave them what I knew and after we had kicked it around a bit, David said, 'Well, if he's Belgian or claims to be, the Belgian authorities can take it over, that's why Frank Lemaire's here. He may have conned you but he's not worth wasting your time on. That O.K. by you, Frank?'

'Sure and if we can establish that he was a collaborator we'll fix him for that at the same time.'

David stood up. 'Where is he? In the nick?'

'Yes, he's on his own. I've released the girl. She was Hungarian and I've handed her over to their repatriation team.'

21

'Well, why not get one of your boys to take Frank down to see Berger.'

And that is what we did.

*   *   *

David settled back in his chair and looked at his refilled glass while he twiddled it around. He was my link with the MI6 liaison team and I'd wondered why he was bothering with friend Berger – but I knew I'd hear when he was ready. We talked for a while about mutual friends, and then he said casually, 'Ever thought of staying on in the racket?'

'No, never – at least not lately.'

'Why?'

'Oh, enough's enough I suppose.'

'Nothing more than that?'

'Well, we are getting a bit like the Krauts, you know.'

'How come?'

'Well, all these bods I send up to 21 AG – we interrogate them, then you interrogate them, and then they just lie around Westertimke – no trial – they'll just rot there till someone gets around to how much it's costing the tax-payer.'

David grinned. 'The Krauts are paying the costs, boyo – you're sure it's not more than that?' And this time he wasn't looking at me like an old mate, but like Major Law – on duty. 'We're moving you to Brunswick, Ted, and we're seconding you to MI6 – you're wasted here.'

'When?'

'Soon as you can – days, not weeks.'

'What to do?'

'CI officer.' He saw the faint response and smiled. 'Yes, you're right, it's a major posting – congratulations.'

'Thanks, what shall I be doing?'

'We want you to run the whole of the line-crossing operation across the border – line-crossers, agents, couriers – the lot.

'What's Bob Fraser going to do?'

'Bob's in the nick in Warsaw – went in six weeks ago.' He leaned forward and he looked suddenly tired. 'Ted, it's a bloody shambles, the whole area is falling to pieces. There are thirteen identified Russian divisions around Magdeburg alone, armour, infantry, artillery – the works. Our people are completely demoralized. We haven't a clue why the Russians are there. Plenty of rumours but nothing reliable. Every move we've made gets clobbered. The Americans are being cagey but they're talking about an invasion in the autumn. The FO think it's all a bluff, or just pressure for a deal. There's a dozen well worked out theories, and just a few real facts could make a hell of a lot of difference. You can have what you want in people and equipment.'

'Why me?'

'First your experience, and second, it's going to take original thinking to get this back on the rails quickly, and third – so's you don't get a big head – there's nobody else we can spare.'

I needed to stand up so I did. I knew just what it must be like over in the Russian Zone – money running short, no instructions, cover stories falling apart and a strong inclination to fade away and go home to Mother.

'Who's taking over here?'

'Mac.'

Captain MacEwen was ten times better an administrator than I was but my heart sank when I thought of my unmilitary professors and crooks being turned into real soldiers after escaping for so long. David guessed what I was thinking and managed a smile. 'They'll survive, my boy – if you've trained 'em right.' And of course they would.

*　　　*　　　*

Two days later I was in Brunswick with those lovely crowns weighing heavy on my shoulders. I'd taken Jacko and the CSM along with me. I'd only been a major two hours when it dawned on me that guards would present arms in future, not just smack their rifles.

There was only one place with real guards for miles, 17 Div HQ three miles away. I didn't know a soul there but it was only three miles. As I walked through the gates, they did it.

CHAPTER FIVE

It took three days to skim through the files and check the existing operation. It was well worked out and administered, over-administered if anything. Too many people in the know and it could take six months to find the leak. There was only one thing to do – start again from scratch. So I called to Jacko and we headed off to 21 AG at Bad Oynhausen. I drew $50,000 U.S. in small notes from David Law. He didn't bat an eye or ask a question, and while we were waiting for it to come he asked if I wanted anything else.

'David, there's a leak somewhere and I haven't got time to find it. I'm going to let all the old network die off. If any of them come back they'll go to the Brunswick house and I'd like you to deal with them. But don't send any of them back into my area, and make clear we've called it a day. I want ten line-crossers from the pool.'

David looked horrified. 'Christ, Ted, we've only got about fifteen for the whole BAOR area.'

I interrupted: 'David, I want four as cut-outs, you can have at least five bods back in three months' time, so as to give this operation maximum security, even internally. I want an assurance that there will be no records kept here and nobody to know what's going on except you. No questions asked. I just get the dope. If it works we carry on – if it doesn't, you clobber me.'

David was silent for several minutes except for tapping his pencil on the edge of his desk, then he reached for the phone and before he picked it up he said: 'It's good sense, Ted – you're quite right, but I must clear it with the DDMI.'

I nodded, and he lifted the phone and pressed the scrambler button.

'I've got our friend here, sir, just over for a chat – no, the other fellow – that's it, sir. He wants to make this a complete cut-out both inside and outside. I think he's right. Will you agree to that, sir?' He listened for a few minutes, nodding his head from time to time. 'Thank you, sir. Yes, I'll tell him – Roger.'

He plonked down the phone and leaned back. 'It's O.K., he agrees – says to give you a good mark. Two exceptions though – we've got to put Joe Steiner in the picture and you've got to give some sort of accounting for the money in due course.'

This was fair enough. Joe Steiner was in charge of all Russian Zone intelligence covering military matters – order of battle, weapons and so on. He was solid as a rock and we had worked together before.

'Fine, David, there's a few more things that I want.'

'Shoot.'

'I'm leaving the Brunswick house, I'm sure it's blown. I want a house in the woods near Helmstedt, it's called the Walderhof. Here's the map reference and I'd like you to get NAAFI to take it over as a rest place. I want two radio operators. I'd like a German-speaking operator from Signals for the house and I want a genuine German operator for over the border.'

David frowned 'The German operator's not easy – you got anyone in mind?'

'Yes, I sent you an Abwehr operator about two months ago, he'd be O.K. His name was Otto Sander.'

'Bit of a risk, isn't it?'

'Not really. I delayed sending him to 21 AG for a few days so that he could get married – she was in the family way – she's the hold on him for us, she lives in Peine.'

David agreed to fix everything I wanted. By the time I got back to Brunswick I had it all worked out in my mind. Mid-evening David phoned to say the house in the woods was available from tomorrow. He'd rustled up three ex-SOE Fanys who would look after the domestic bits for us.

Three days later we were installed in the Walderhof. Joe Steiner came down and gave a four-day briefing to my motley crew. Most of the documents were genuine and we

25

went over the cover stories and the routines until I was satisfied. To give them confidence I was drawing them back after a week and this would give me the chance of sorting them out and giving them a pep talk. They were individually housed at various military units in the area and that was where they would report back in a week. They were not going to meet their cut-outs for their first contact until after the first trip. The cut-outs would be left in the field and I would be their contact so nobody would connect back to the little grey house in the woods.

*   *   *

After they came back from the first trip, it took a week to do the rounds although Joe Steiner helped. They had done very well and it gave them confidence. We duly shoved them off again and they knew they would see me at least once a month over the other side.

Discussing it after they had gone, David and Joe seemed pleased. Joe had some dope about transport that seemed to fit in and please him. They were calling back at Hildesheim on the way home and took my regards to the boys.

For two days nothing happened and the radio operation over the border didn't come on net at any of the arranged times. By the third day, I was half wishing I had arranged one compulsory nil report, despite the risk, and then at 1800 hours we got the first stuff and then it kept coming in nicely. No pretty pictures but lots of jig-saw pieces that Joe's outfit could put together.

We did four months of this and it went like clockwork. I had done seven trips across, taking money, instructions and encouragement. Everyone was very pleased except me. I was dead tired and apprehensive. In this kind of game luck didn't last too long and I wondered where the blow would fall, and I had half a mind to call them all back for a week's rest. Jacko looked after the dollar exchange on the black market and we weren't going to need more money for at least another two months. The day before I was due to cross again, David phoned and said that both he and the DDMI wanted me to miss the trip. I couldn't do this or it

26

would start the rot. They must have known this. They insisted I put the crossing back by two days. I couldn't tell whether they knew something or were just being cautious. I agreed and took it easy for two days.

CHAPTER SIX

I had crossed the border at my usual place and was standing on the edge of the woods. There had been a short summer rainstorm but the sun was shining now. The forest gave on to a broad sloping field lit by the sunshine and with a light mist rising from the hot earth. If you walk through wet grass it leaves a track for days. I had plenty of time and the grass would dry in half an hour so I stood and enjoyed the peaceful scene. It reminded me of Beethoven's 'Pastoral' – after the storm. Raindrops hung and dripped from the leaves above me and along the edges of the field were poppies and cornflowers. For no good reason I remembered that cornflowers were Bismarck's favourite flower. There were generally sheep grazing in the field with a boy watching over them but today the field was empty and it looked as if it had not been grazed for several days. There were wood pigeons calling and a blackbird was singing very near. It felt good to be alive. I was wearing a blue serge suit and the bottoms of the trousers were wet and I bent over to look – and everything went red, then black.

When I came to I was looking up a tall green tree and there was a man's head on it and then the green tree became a man's leg and the green was the uniform of the Grenzpolizei. The man was standing on my hand. He was talking to another man and I heard: '... die sind trotzdem die zuständige Behörde.'

The other fellow nodded and there was the noise of a man walking through the undergrowth and they both turned towards the newcomer. The fellow with his boot on my hand said 'Zravstvuyte'. The third man nodded back as he looked down at me. He was wearing an NKVD uniform and they had thought it worth while sending a colonel. I didn't like that. He looked at my man. 'Er war allein?'

'Ja, Herr Oberst, es war genau wie Sie gesagt haben.'

28

He gave the enthusiast a dirty look and told him to shut up. They had expected me and that made me feel very cold indeed. Frontier police I didn't mind. NKVD – well, fifty-fifty. But NKVD who expected me, that was a horse of another stripe. I kind of wished the man's boot would stay on my hand for a long time. The colonel looked down on me, hands on hips, but he said nothing and through the ache at the back of my head I could hear the birds again. Then I heard the distant noise of a truck heading our way along the edge of the woods and finally it stopped near by. Four Russian privates arrived, sweating and saluting. Their uniforms were old and patched and I wondered if it ever crossed their minds that if all were equal, why they were so scruffy and the officers so smart. There were smiles and grins all round and everyone was obviously delighted, except me. Then comrade colonel kicked my feet, not in spite but identification, 'Aufstehen.' And suddenly I knew I'd got a chance. I was expected, but he spoke in German, if they knew who I was he'd have spoken in English.

When I stood up, I was sick, and the sky moved and the ground tilted. Two of them helped me over to the truck. We bounced across the edge of the fields, down to a cart track, past some farm buildings and on to the main road to Mag-deburg. I tried hard to hold on to my mind and my glimmer of hope made up for the pain in my head and my neck. I realized now why the boy with the sheep wasn't there. When we swung right at Charlotten Allee I knew we were headed for the NKVD HQ which was the old Gestapo HQ in Rupprechtstrasse. When we stopped I clambered down and they took me straight down the steps to the basement. Then into a corridor, past cells, and into a large room with stone walls and no window. There was a large kitchen table and a bare bulb swinging from the ceiling.

The colonel opened his mouth to speak to me but was interrupted by another officer who stood just inside the door. He was talking very fast, too fast for my Russian, but I sensed there was some sort of panic on. The colonel nod-ded from time to time, then, with a curt 'Da, da', he waved the other fellow out and turned to face me. His face was close to mine and he looked at me as if he wanted to examine every inch of my face. My legs were trembling and I couldn't stop them, I just wanted to lie down. He rocked gently on his heels and then, very quietly but very clearly, he said in English:

'Well, Major Bailey, I'm afraid we're in a hurry.'

He knew – he'd known all along. He'd just done it the expert's way – built me up for the big knock-down. He gestured to one of the chairs and I sat down, but it seemed to take a long time for my brain to send messages to my arms and legs. He was too smooth to put his chair on the other side of the table and create a division at this stage. He pulled a chair so that we were facing each other. It was like some sort of love-seat, except that he stretched out his legs, undid two jacket buttons and leaned back comfortably, and looked me over. His eyes went to my hand and mine followed. It was dirty and caked with blood where the boot studs had scuffed away the skin. Our eyes met. His were brown but they weren't gentle, but clear and brown like an eagle's eyes. Missing nothing.

'Well, Major Bailey, let's get started.'

I shook my head. 'Leider sprech' ich kein Englisch.'

He pursed his lips impatiently and shrugging his shoulders, spoke in German. He seemed at home in English but he had to sort out his words first in German, which gave me a slight edge. But you'd have needed a micrometer to measure it. My cover story was that I was Theo Birkemeir from Göttingen, industrial photographer, unable to get a permanent MilGov licence to operate, finally trying my luck over the border. No idea what the conditions were like and no idea of how to go about it. I had an Arbeitsamt-registration, ration cards and identity card.

The colonel took all the documents and glanced at them, with no great interest.

'This address in Göttingen. When were you last there?'

He walked over to a desk and took out a pad and fished in his pocket and pulled out a pen.

'This morning, Colonel. I left at six o'clock.'

'How do you know I'm a colonel?'

'The man called you Colonel.'

'Why didn't you go to the check-point and come in that way?'

'I did. My name will be registered there but the guard told me I needed an Ausweis, and I must apply through Hanover, and it would take two or three months, at least.'

'Who showed you the way?'

'Nobody.'

'Who were you waiting for?'

'Nobody, I was just waiting after the storm.'

'Who is your contact in Magdeburg?'

'I have no contacts, Colonel, I'm a stranger to these parts – I don't know them at all.'

He walked over to a large-scale map on the wall and waved me over to him. He put his pen on the edge of a patch of green. 'This is where you were arrested, show me how you got there.'

That was an old dodge – whatever you said showed you could read an ordnance survey map. I frowned at the map for a few moments and then gave up. 'I can't read these things, Colonel.'

We walked back to the chairs together and when he had settled down again, 'Look, Bailey, or Birkemeir, whatever you choose to call yourself, we both know it's just a question of time before you tell us what we want to know. We already know most of it so you might as well co-operate. There won't be any rescue parties for you, no more than there were for Herr Fraser. You have the choice – you can talk it over with me or I'll pass you over to my colleagues in Section 4. You know the facts of life – we're both in the same business.'

'I wish I could help you, Colonel, but I can't. Is it possible to send a message to my home?'

He smiled coldly. 'I should think Joe Steiner knows already, but it won't make any difference either way – to him, to me or to you.'

They were bound to know a lot about Joe, but for a guy in a hurry, he seemed very confident all round. He stood up, stuffed his pen back in his pocket and picked up my papers and his pad. With his hands on the table he leaned across, 'Major Bailey, we picked up your operator Otto Sander this morning, and we have his code pad. Give me the schedule and the wavelength and I personally guarantee that we will take you back to the border and let you pass over freely.'

He waited a long time, and then without another word, he walked over to the door, called to the guard outside and the heavy key turned and he went out. They knew who I was all right or at least they knew who I could be, and it was obvious why they were in a hurry. They wanted to operate the radio and turn the operation back on us.

At the hotel in Matlock and the house near Oxford we had gone through countless rehearsals of how to behave when caught and under interrogation. It was all good stuff, but it was a long time ago, and it was all designed for being caught by Italians or Germans. Nobody had thought then about being put in the bag by our gallant Allies. We know a lot about the various ploys and methods of German interrogation, but we didn't know much about the Russians. But we had seen them at work in Berlin, in public, and we didn't need much telling after that. The information on the boys of Section 4 was pretty scant. The NKVD were no ladies and they left to Section 4 what they didn't fancy doing themselves. All told it would be safe to say that the types in Section 4 didn't go much for Tchaikovsky or Rachmaninov.

Although I had interrogated a lot of people myself, the experience didn't seem to help now that my turn had come around. The impossibility, the indignity, were more powerful than I expected. It wasn't going to be a battle of wits, but a dull, bad dream and at first I just worried about what was happening back at the Walderhof. I was like a housewife on holiday fretting about whether she'd turned the gas off. I was impatient to get back. My head was much better and after about half an hour on my own, I looked around the room. There was the big heavy kitchen table which was clamped to the concrete floor. Half a dozen solid chairs. A small desk. Heavy-duty power points here and there. A small sink with a dripping tap. The big map on the wall and that was about it. Not a home from home, but I was feeling much fitter and generally perky.

There was a noise of heavy boots in the corridor and a few moments later the door swung open and three men came in. The biggest, who was very big, surveyed me from the area of the door which the others were closing. He wore cavalry breeches and soft leather jack-boots. A shirt that was open to the waist and he slowly rolled up his sleeves. He wore one of those wide leather wrist bands that bully boys so often seem to wear as a badge of office. His head was close shaven and his right ear looked as though it had melted. I was built on the large side myself but this man was at least four inches taller and twenty-five pounds heavier. Even forgetting his two mates he had a lot of advantages. But I had one – a grim one, but a real one. The sooner I was unconscious the better. They were in a hurry and they needed me conscious and able to talk, and I had no intention of sitting around while they worked me over. I was standing a few feet in front of the table and he said in atrocious German, 'All we want is radio times and frequency.'

I didn't answer and he came forward at me, right arm lifted to bash my face. I side-stepped, grabbed the solid arm and he went over my thigh like a lamb, and the big bullet head crashed against the fixed table leg. I reached for a chair and went for his mates. It was a good solid chair and number one went down screaming and I went after number two who went under the chair and drove me back against the wall. Then he and the big fellow were all over me and we fought like wild-cats along the wall to the door. Then one of them chopped at my neck from the back and my left arm was finished and my feet didn't touch as they threw me at the table. The edge gave my spine a sickening blow and they had me pinned down, a leg and an arm apiece. The big fellow gasped something in Russian and one of them gripped my hand and I felt him press my little finger to the edge of the table and I heard it crack as the pain flooded through me, then the same thing happened to my thumb.

I seemed to be floating gently backwards on a soft bed, and it was Sunday at grandma's and she was breaking the leg of a chicken so that she could cut me a slice of the breast. And then it was dark and we were standing at the small sink in the scullery under the gas lamp and grandma was gently washing my face. I could hear grandpa outside cleaning the shoes and singing 'Father O'Flynn', and grandma said 'Close your eyes, Sunbeam, and you won't get the soap in them,' and then the water was cold and too much and I came to, and a bowl of water flooded my face and my head came up gasping. My left eye was closed but I could see the light bulb swinging up above me. Then my senses came back. I could see the big one and his pal resting and the other one seemed to have gone. Then they got up and started on me again and I was out in no time. This happened a number of times and twice when I was conscious I was in the room on my own, but I couldn't move. It felt like I was on fire and my heart was beating in my mouth and my legs and my hands, and there seemed to be blood all over my chest and shoulders. I could just raise my head and a lot of blood came out of my mouth and the ceiling came down on my face.

When I next surfaced, the colonel was there bending over me, and to my surprise he put his arm under my head, and lifting it quite gently he cleaned my face with a towel. He eased my body down so that my head was on the table and said 'We'll settle for the frequency – I think you've had enough.'

He was right – I had. It's only in books that they bash you for days and you don't say a word.

'How long have I been here?'

'A couple of days.'

It wasn't quite long enough and anyway it might not be true. Say another four hours. With no radio traffic and no me for two days, even 21 AG would get the message. One more session would do it. The colonel looked very clean and tidy and indeed hopeful. One more session and I'd talk – anything they wanted. So I looked at him with my one good eye, and he waited – and I said 'Get stuffed' in English. A slight frown and then he'd worked it out and flushed with anger. He called out and the heavenly twins came in, wiping their mouths with the backs of their hands. They had quite a long chat in Russian, and mate went over to the sink and filled the bowl with water and shoved the bloody towel under the tap. I could hardly believe they were going to clean me up, but it looked remarkably like it. The wet towel went over my face and then they poured on the water. For a long, long time I drowned and surfaced. When it was almost too late and my lungs were bursting they lifted the towel and my throat strained and heaved to pull in air and I could hear the terrible groaning noise the sea-lions make at feeding time. It filled the room and it was me.

When I came round I was in one of the cells and the sun shone through a high window above me. The cell was long and narrow and quite empty and despite the sun it was very cold and I was shivering. I must have been there quite a time because all the blood was dry and dark-brown.

      *   *   *

I gathered that it was some military celebration for the Russian Army the day I escaped, and I was so stupid and clobbered that I went back over the border at my usual crossing.

21 Army Group decided I needed at least two weeks in hospital for observation, and I had a shrewd idea they needed time to make up their minds whether I had been 'got at' or not.

CHAPTER SEVEN

The conference hall was a small building standing on its own in the compound. It was, in fact, one room of polished pine-wood with a single door and no windows. Its occupants could never be observed from the outside; it was completely sound-proof and subject to a twenty-four-hour electronic surveillance.

By today's sophisticated standards the security was extremely primitive. It was, nevertheless, the best that Combined Security Forces could provide at that time. Four Field Security sergeants guarded its barbed wire perimeter. Inside, apart from two ceiling lights and two standard-issue army trestles and chairs, there was no furniture and no decoration, except two photographs, one of King George VI and the famous Karsh photograph of Churchill.

At the head of the table was the Deputy Director of Military Intelligence, Colonel Jackson. He was a full colonel and by far the most experienced soldier in the room. On the other hand he was the least experienced intelligence man, for, like most DDMIs he had been seconded from normal army duties to serve as an administrator of the wilder elements that came under the heading of Intelligence or Security.

In Colonel Jackson, 30 Corps were extremely lucky. He had been an extremely successful Royal Artillery officer and felt no need to concern himself too deeply with the day-to-day operations which he referred to casually as 'the general carryings on.'

On his right was a civilian – the MI6 representative James Broadbent; Eton, Trinity and the Guards Club.

On his left was Joe Steiner who looked like a battered version of Spencer Tracy but whose mind was as crisp as Lenin's which was all to the good because Major Steiner was responsible to 21 Army Group for all information covering the Russian occupied zone of Germany.

The others were Major David Law, representing 30 Corps counter-intelligence, two men who ranked only as 'in attendance' – a civilian Foreign Office representative named Lawden, and the British Army of the Rhine liaison officer to the Russian mission in the British Zone – Captain Remak. Facing the DDMI at the other end of the trestle tables was Major Cowan of the Judge Advocate's department.

'Well, gentlemen,' the DDMI said, 'we all know why we are here and that's to discuss the case of Major Bailey. You've seen all the available documents, the de-briefing report, Major Bailey's own statement, the medical report and as assessment of the situation by Major Law of 30 Corps. Subject, of course, to anything that Major Cowan may have to tell us or advise us, I feel I should start by making clear that this is not a court-martial, or even a court of inquiry. This officer is not on trial in any way. We're simply here to assess this particular situation so that we can take the necessary action for this officer to continue his career in one direction or another.

'At the same time, we are concerned that any action we may propose does not do harm to the security of the British occupying forces or their allies and, of course, by this I mean their Western allies. Putting it at its crudest level, we have to decide whether in our opinion this young officer, who underwent severe physical mistreatment whilst a prisoner, talked or did not talk. If the feeling is that he talked, we have to assess how much he talked – what information he gave away. It would also be sensible to bear in mind that if this officer did talk or co-operate in any way with his captors, it is also possible that his escape was contrived and that either voluntarily or under pressure he is now working for the Russian intelligence service. Our colleagues here from MI6 and the Foreign Office are interested parties because you will recall that during this operation Major Bailey was seconded as a civilian to MI6. Major Cowan from the Judge Advocate's department is here to see that we don't get our legal lines crossed whatever decision we may make. Perhaps Major Law would like to start the ball rolling.' Then catching sight of a waving hand, the DDMI looked around and said, 'I see that Major Cowan has something he would like to say.'

'There is a point that I think I should make, sir, before you start your deliberations. If your verdict – if your decision – should turn out to be that this officer has given information to the Russians or, alternatively, is now being used by the Russians, it may be that you would decide to send the papers in this case for legal handling to my department. So, it may be worth while establishing right from the beginning the importance that we should attach to the possibility of prior collusion with the Russians. So could we clearly establish whether this officer volunteered for this work or was given a direct order.'

Colonel Jackson nodded as if in agreement with this thinking and turned to Major Law. 'David, where do we stand on that point?'

'Well, sir, there's no doubt on this point at all. I gave him a direct order that he was to undertake this work. I would, of course, have allowed him to decline, but he didn't. He was very reluctant to leave his unit but, after some persuasion from me, he undertook the assignment. There is no question at all that this was by direct order from me.'

'Thank you, David, now perhaps you could carry on and put us in the picture.'

David Law leaned back comfortably and, with his head resting on the back of his chair, stared at the ceiling.

'When this assignment started, we were extremely worried about the build-up of all types of Russian forces in the Magdeburg area. An appreciation from the Combined Services Intelligence Unit went so far as to suggest the possibility of the Russian armed forces launching an attack across the border. Our network in the area had been completely broken up and the remains were not operational in any sensible meaning of the word. This officer set up a new network which was completely secure, and for several months sent us back information which allowed us to draw conclusions that were subsequently found to be correct. The network and the officer-in-charge, whom we're now discussing, worked extremely intensively and, as the information they passed became more conclusive, other interested departments and sections tended to overload the network with excessive demands. Until a few days before this officer's capture we had no indications that the network was insecure or that it had been penetrated. However, two days before Bailey's capture, one of Joe Steiner's sources of information indicated that the NKVD was aware of the names and duties of a number of counter-intelligence officers responsible for operations into the Russian Zone. No actual names had been given this informant, but he was under the impression that they included names of officers of 21 Army Group and 30 Corps. You will see from Bailey's own statement that there is some corroboration there – for what it's worth. It's also worth noting that although the Russians told Bailey that they had captured his radio operator, Sander, they had not, in fact, done so. The whole operation has been suspended and is now in the charge of Major Steiner and for the moment we are only getting low-level information from an American CIC network, operating out of Kassel.'

The MI6 representative looked across at David Law and, seeing that he had finished talking, asked, 'Would it be possible for Major Steiner to indicate the reliability of his informant.'

Joe Steiner looked at the DDMI and, seeing his acquiescent nod, he said, 'The source has always been absolutely reliable and I don't think there is any reason why I shouldn't tell you that it's a senior NKVD officer, Russian father, Polish mother. Apart from this, there was some secondary information via Captain Remak. He might like to tell you about that himself.'

'Well,' began the BAOR officer, Remak, 'during the month prior to this officer being taken prisoner, the Russian Army liaison unit and particularly Major Polokoff were very pressing about inviting particular officers to various parties that they were giving. They seemed particularly interested in Joe Steiner and David Law. They weren't the only names they mentioned, of course, but I had the feeling that the others were just a cover-up and that it was really David and Joe they wanted to meet. I reported this to Major Steiner at the time and I understand that he informed Major Law.'

Joe Steiner leaned forward with his arms on the table. 'Yes, I can confirm that this was reported to me and perhaps I had better clear up one or two other points. As soon as Bailey was caught, I withdrew the whole of the network, including the radio operators, and they've all been at the Deep Interrogation Centre at Westertimke and, in fact, they're still there. They've all been processed and there's no indication that they were penetrated or uncovered; in fact, they went on operating for thirty-six hours after Bailey was caught before I could pull them out. As far as I'm concerned, they're all suitable for further employment providing it's not across the border.'

Remak spoke up again. 'I think it's also worth pointing out, sir, that the Russians have not shown any interest in either Joe or David since Bailey was caught or since he escaped. They've given one or two parties since then which I've attended, and I arranged for one of our security officers who's being demobbed to attend a party with me posing as Joe Steiner and, although we were under the impression that a photograph was taken, they didn't appear to be particularly interested.'

The DDMI patted together his papers and, looking round the table, said, 'Well, gentlemen, could I have your opinions?'

David Law pushed his hands through his hair and, with something of a sigh, said, 'I suppose I ought to go first and it's my assessment that this officer gave no information to the Russians and was not turned by them. My knowledge of the officer concerned, and all the evidence we have available, points that way. Nevertheless, because I can't be sure, I recommend that Bailey be given appropriate sick leave and if he is not then due for demobilization, he should be seconded to GHQ Home Forces and should be given some non-active assignment. The kind of thing I have in mind is a manual on operating an information network.'

Joe Steiner, looking very judicial, said, 'I agree with David's assessment and I agree with his recommendations.'

The DDMI was thoughtful for a few moments and then said, 'Well, gentlemen, I agree with your conclusions, but one thing does disturb me. We are all of the opinion that this officer did not give information to his captors and it seems to me that we are rewarding him ill for his efforts. Apart from the work which he did, which I assume you are treating as being in the line of duty, he was, in fact, most brutally treated, and you will see from the medical report that he sustained a number of fractures, none of them major, but all of them extremely painful. There is also some reference, in medical terms which I can't understand completely, to injuries to the nerve centres controlling the windpipe. If you'll also bear in mind the opinion of the two psychiatrists involved that this event is almost certain to give rise to disadvantageous psychological repercussions later in life, we seem to be coming to the conclusion that this young man did an exceptional job of work, resisted extreme physical pressures and, as a mark of our appreciation, we send him off into some backwater. I should like to suggest that, at least, we give him a promotion.'

David Law pursed his lips, and looking rather unhappy slowly shook his head. 'We can't really do that, sir, he had a promotion when he was given this assignment.'

Mr Lawden of the Foreign Office who, up to now, had said nothing, stretched his arms with obvious boredom, and no little condescension, and said, 'I noticed in Bailey's "P" file that he comes from a working-class background, he's pretty tough and he's been doing this kind of work for a good number of years now, and I can't see that he's likely to come to any great harm psychologically or otherwise. Don't you think, perhaps, we're making a bit too much of a fuss about him?'

The DDMI flushed and looked down at his papers. 'Mr Lawden – it is Lawden, isn't it? – I find your comment unpleasant and unhelpful. I hope that it's not ignorant also, and perhaps you could tell us on what experience or information your comment was based.'

Broadbent, the MI6 man, rushed in to divert the military wrath from his fellow civilian. 'What about giving him a decoration, sir, a DSO or something like that?'

The DDMI didn't like the 'or something like that' bit at all.

Joe Steiner and David Law knew it and waited for the explosion, but the DDMI was too old a hand to be baited by a couple of whippersnappers from Whitehall and, looking at nobody in particular, he said, 'I think that's an excellent suggestion, Mr Broadbent, a good solution and I'll put forward the recommendation myself. And now,' he said looking at the two civilians, 'perhaps I could invite you all to have a drink with me in the Mess.'

And that was the end of that.

CHAPTER EIGHT

I was actually in hospital for about three weeks. I'd been moved out of Germany and stuck in a special hospital wing at Fresnes in Paris. It's worth mentioning for those who don't know, that Fresnes is a prison, and it was much loved by the Gestapo. The warders are all out of Dumas and have served dozens of authorities with all the efficiency of French bureaucracy at its best.

I gathered that they had put me up for a 'gong' and I gathered that I probably wouldn't get it. After three weeks I stayed with friends in Paris and life was better. I was asked if I'd like to stay in the 'firm', I declined and got my discharge papers and was demobbed at Hull complete with brown trilby, chalk-striped suit, which came back into fashion after Bonnie and Clyde, and sundry underwear. I was not an immediate success in civvy street, a series of girls and one wife who couldn't stand that my feet wiggled in bed when I was dreaming bad dreams. I can't blame them; nobody had ever hurt my feet and they worked like a two-stroke engine. Like anybody who has been in the racket, I still had a tendency when visiting friends to look the place over and wonder how to get out, and an immovable inclination to sit with my back to a wall and not facing a window. I heard on the grape-vine that my old friend Berger, despite the Belgian authorities, had feigned appendicitis and then skipped out of the prison hospital, so he was happy.

When you leave one of the intelligence agencies there is an odd period of about six months when you know what's going to be in the papers before it gets there and then suddenly you don't know any more than the guy next door. You're better at reading between the lines, but on East–West matters the lines are printed fairly close together. After five years of civilian life I'd pretty well forgotten it all – the war, the old firm – except that whenever I was under a real emotional stress an odd thing happened. The first time it happened was at the Royal Aero Club. The divorce had just started and in the middle of lunch my windpipe sort of collapsed and I stood up in a panic and I heard those sea-lion noises all over again. Senior Air Force officers tried to get on with their steaks as if the dining-room was always filled with this terrible noise. An RAF doctor took me outside and just as I felt I was a 'gonner' it simply righted itself and I was trembling, soaked in sweat and blaming it on a piece of melon. After that it happened about once a year. When it happened in the car it was panic stations to stop and get out and lean on a wall. Considering that it was a pretty loud noise nobody paid much attention except well-dressed middle-class ladies, who would say in their authoritative voices, 'Absolutely disgusting – and in the morning too.' My own doctor had said that if I could fight the panic it would ease quickly if I could get to fresh air and, she added, 'It's at least 60 to 40 against it being fatal.' I didn't feel those were the best odds available, but for my annual 'happening' I gradually found a formula that seemed to work.

It was in November 1939 that I had been recruited into counter-intelligence at an interview at the back of a barber's shop in Trafalgar Square mainly on the basis of my foreign languages, which were adequate rather than good, and I can remember the full colonel who finally said 'yes' telling me how lucky I was.

'You'll find you've joined a very fine club my boy, bring your sports kit and your car – we'll see you get enough petrol coupons – and you'll find we'll teach you a lot – it'll help you after this war's over. Be good experience.'

I had gathered during the various interviews that my background had been well researched and I wasn't too impressed, because in 1939 twenty-year-old boys from the back streets of Birmingham had probably never been in a car, let alone owned one. For me, I had just bought my first bicycle, second-hand for a pound. But the old boy was right, it was a kind of exclusive club and I fitted in well. Most of the other guys were university professors or lecturers or whatever, but I soon realized there was a difference between education and intelligence: to my disbelief and pleasure I found that I could think better than they could. They seemed confined to straight lines by their academic disciplines, and my ignorance allowed or compelled 360-degree thinking. Apart from that I had a strong streak of feminine intuition and that gave me a high survival factor. Anyway the outfit suited me and I suited it. It taught me a lot – some practical things and a lot about people.

So when the war was all over it took me some time to sort out being a civilian, but I soon decided to leave my Birmingham background and through selling and management I gravitated to advertising.

Soon after I was back I married the 'girl I left behind me'. The marriage guidance counsellor subsequently asked me how long we had known one another before we married and the answer was five years, but it wasn't really true because for all of those years we hadn't seen each other for more than ten days all told. Nobody did anything wrong and she was an excellent wife, except if I kissed her she always offered me her cheek. She was very pretty and it lasted two years and the break-up was all my fault. I met Sally and she kissed me on the mouth and for the first time in my life I knew what it was like to be loved. Being loved by Sally was like being in a permanent warm bath with lots of Badedas, listening to Max Bruch's fiddle concerto, eating éclairs and meringues and mentally reciting Palgrave's Golden Treasury. For the first time in my life I felt loved and for the first time in my life I realized what it was like not to be lonely. Divorces could take quite a time in those days, in this case about eighteen months; Sally and I lived together in our warm sunny world. When adultery is the grounds for divorce 'the other woman' is referred to in legal terms as the 'woman named', and if it's undefended and the money bit is sorted out it's done by the thousand a year, like shelling peas. There was nothing extraordinary about my divorce except that when it was heard the 'woman named' had been dead for six weeks. I suppose there must have been one day in the last twenty years when I haven't thought about Sally, but I don't recall it.

My wartime training had concentrated on getting into other people's minds and an absolute instinct for when people were telling lies. This had a good many advantages in the advertising business but was not a social asset and I did my best not to let it get in the way of personal relationships. The bells rang for the lies, but you ignored them and in the end I suppose you get to the stage when you not only abandon a trained hypersensitivity but you go to the other extreme and ignore what any normal man would notice.

About three years after Sally died I won an advertising award which not only upped my status and salary but I was interviewed for one of the trade magazines. When I agreed to this interview I might just as well have flown to Moscow and knocked on that small green door half-way down the second turning on the right going down the Kalinina Prospekt – the home of Section 4 of the KGB. It made what happened in Magdeburg seem like a Sunday-school treat. It's got nothing to do with spies or counter-spies – or very little; but in a way it's got everything to do with both, because nobody seems to realize that spies and counter-spies aren't always busy at their work, they have homes, they love people, they get jobs – because it's all over when you're about forty. And some work it all out and some don't.

CHAPTER NINE

The interview was over lunch at my club. The Special Forces Club is in one of the small streets off the top end of Sloane Street and it's quiet and homely, and the members are ex-SOE, SAS and all the other private armies, and unless we have another war soon, it's going to run out of members.

The girl was about thirty, a not very experienced freelance, who normally wrote two-guinea pieces for the provincials on the latest thing at the Tate and that sort of jazz. We went through the usual routine and covered the back streets to riches bit, and she'd read up my war bit and we discussed my prize-winning ad at more length than it was worth. The whole lot didn't get us past the soup and somehow we got on to the subject of Scott Fitzgerald, we were both fans of his but we disagreed about Zelda. I always thought Zelda was a pain in the neck, that she turned a writer into a drunk and always sought the limelight because she was jealous of his real talent, and from the pictures she didn't look any great beauty anyway. The girl thought she was Fitzgerald's inspiration and we left it at that. By the 'sole bonne femme' we were talking about her. Daddy was a diamond merchant from one of the banana republics and the family had dragged its little circus round most of the European capitals. The kids had been brought up by nannies and had only seen the parents at bed-time, for a pat on the head and a quick look at Mama in her ball gown. She had two honours degrees in languages and had married a rising politician from the banana republic and her name was Lara. She'd lit out from the husband and two daughters a year ago. He, apparently, was a domestic tyrant, and she'd got out from under when his father, who just happened to be Lord Chief Justice, had suggested she might like to have a rest in the local mental home.

She wasn't wildly pretty but was attractive, or could be if

she relaxed. The grey-blue eyes looked haunted, and she'd obviously had a bad time. We had a lot in common, languages, literature – the usual stuff – and as she told me about her life in the small capital, I was impressed by her truthfulness. I care a lot, perhaps too much, about truthfulness, and this girl didn't spare herself. Her married life had not been good and the long series of tatty and furtive affairs and heavy drinking had obviously brought no joy and no love and in the end she'd left it all, to start again.

When you do that you expect the Good Lord to give you a small prize, but so far it was only another tatty affair with a copy-writer who was happily married with three kids. I decided on some instinct to take over from God, and we ate that evening at Grosvenor House, and the only argument we ever had in our lives was whether we met on the 30th or 31st November. We went around together most days for the next three weeks and affection and sympathy soon became love. The copy-writer was dealt with while I was in Los Angeles for two days. It apparently led to scenes and tears the like of which had not been seen before in the Berkeley Buttery. Then there was the marriage bit. She was in the process of divorcing him but he still wanted her back, and we agreed that she should see him once again to make up her mind. Three weeks later the phone rang in the middle of the night and she'd seen him and decided. She couldn't go back, he was as unreasonable as ever. I walked round to her room and she looked haunted again but kind of elated as if the decision was a complete cure that needed an hour to work through her system. That night was the first time we'd done anything more than kiss, and when I said we'd have to be careful, she gave me a bar to my DSO and said very gently as her arms went round me, 'I couldn't do anything to stop me having a baby of yours.'

I don't think Samantha was conceived at that time but she was born just over nine months later and I loved her with all my heart.

Meantime, back at the ranch-house, as they say, a lot had happened. A letter extolling my virtues had been sent to New York, where Daddy was now operating. Bearing in mind what she'd told me of the background, nobody should have been surprised by the reply. Daddy was going to have my divorce, my war record and my antecedents investigated, and one thing was for sure, 'those whose education ended at fifteen are never capable of learning foreign languages' so that was that. The first Christmas I made a mistake. I bought Lara an expensive coat – it was the only present she had, and from them on I had to remember at Christmas and birthdays to give a lot of small presents. Although she had told me she was not fond of her two daughters because they were the result of enforced conjugal rights I know she somehow grieved at not seeing them and not being allowed to correspond with them. Solicitors' letters said, 'She has done enough harm to them already.' The man was clearly a first-class bastard.

We lived happily and uneventfully for three years. When we were on our own we talked of books and art and politics, but I noticed an odd thing. When friends came we got the saga of high-society, high-living and servants, points were being made not very subtly that we were in the presence of things beyond our ken. This pleasant girl was not just a girl but a creature from the outer space of castles and palaces, a-visiting the mortals. Most people took it in their stride, even third time round, but it sounded like Ruritania in the 'twenties and it made me think of large empty rooms with dusty furniture and rotting tapestries, and I found it slightly disturbing.

Then there was a pleasant surprise. Mama was going to pay us a visit. She was forbidden to actually reside with us, so an elaborate charade was set up with a local hotel. Mama was a charmer, who drank solidly from morning till night and never showed a sign of it. Bottle after bottle went down but there wasn't a slurred word. A great raconteuse she regaled us with how Daddy slammed her in the stomach and she had demanded the doctor; to avoid embarrassment she had been given the trip to see her daughter instead. It could sound a gross exaggeration, but I remembered a letter from her sister on our first year together. She and her husband lived with the parents and they were all

49

forbidden to write to Lara. Any reply had to go back via a sister in Spain, with typewritten address – it sounded like the postal arrangement for dirty pictures. But it seemed that there was 'a regime of terror', and if the correspondence was discovered they would all be thrown on the streets of New York. Anyway Mama drank solidly, and chatted charmingly, and out of a million words the bells rang twice, but I'd trained myself not to listen. Mama said, 'What a pity Lara had never got a degree,' and she talked of a doll's dress she had made for one of Lara's dolls.

That night Lara was drunk and insensible and I carried her up to bed. There's something incongruous about being drunk in a thatched cottage with roses around the door and I looked down at her. The mouth was wide open and she snored stertorously, and her face was haggard and taut. The bones stood out, and the face was that of a bird of prey. I realized her husband must have seen her like this many times.

Three months later there was an invitation to Paris from an old school friend of Lara. I was paying back-tax and we were very broke, so only Lara went. When I got back from Heathrow I went to the nursery to cuddle Samantha and as I passed through our bedroom, the bells rang again. In the waste basket was a torn-up page of paper. Some people tear up paper, some people screw it up, Lara was a screwer-upper. I stuck it together and it had a name and a list of telephone numbers. The name was the copy-writer's and the numbers marked his moves in the last three years. I did a little checking and, yes, he'd gone to Paris. Lara was back on the Tuesday and two weeks later I came home one evening and there was no Lara and no Samantha. No clothes, no jewels. And I was back in Magdeburg. She came back six weeks later.

Six weeks doesn't sound very long but I lost twenty-five pounds in weight and my security. The thought of that fortnight spent talking, loving and living, whilst planning to walk out, sickened me. No complaints, no discussions, just a furtive walk out. At the end of the week was a note from a solicitor asking me to 'place Mrs Bailey's goods in store for her'. There weren't any goods; when I took her over there was nothing but debts, some clothes and a lot of empty whisky bottles. So I wrote her a love letter to come back; maybe the move to the country was the root of it all. The reply was loving – all she wanted to do was come back, all I had to do was say the word. So off went the loving reply. Her next letter said how pleased she was but she was ill and having medical treatment. I was panic-stricken and sank my pride and phoned the people where I guessed she was staying. They were much amused. Lara was fit as a flea, having a great time and was out for the evening and wouldn't be back until the early hours of the morning. I sent a bitter telegram and three weeks later she phoned and came back. You don't need to have had six years in counter-intelligence to read the signs; any normal man would have faced the facts of life. But I didn't. I loved her. I loved Samantha, and I'd crossed the line that makes you listen to the warning bells.

We moved back to London and new friends got the high-living bit, and when she was drunk they got the lot. There were no grounds for divorce from her previous husband, so our Sammy was illegitimate, and they got that, and the wealthy husband and daddy. And our circle of friends got smaller and smaller. It survived two years and then I came back one night again to the empty cupboards. All the clothes, the jewels were gone, but Sammy's toys were there. So Sammy, aged four, was off on the long distance trail. The High Court gave me custody and all that, but Sammy was a long way out of their jurisdiction. I wrote to Mama, and in the end to Lara's father. There were no answers, because they didn't give a damn for people – me, Sammy or anyone else. For long months I was haunted by my thoughts of what would be happening to Sammy. A mother who couldn't look after herself let alone a child, who'd already deserted two daughters.

It was four years before Lara died, and I didn't hear until a year later. Sammy had been abandoned long before but there were no clues as to where she was. I spent my last cent on a hundred false trails but I never got within miles.

CHAPTER TEN

The lights in the 707 flickered. There was a thud as the under-carriage came down and the captain's voice crackled through the passenger radio, 'This is Transworld Airlines flight number 405, Captain O'Casey speaking, we are now coming in to land at Kennedy International Airport. The ground temperature at Kennedy is well down and passengers are warned that there is ice on the tarmac. The crew and I have enjoyed having you aboard and we hope you have enjoyed the flight.'

Something comes out in human beings when an aircraft lands, and despite all the cautions of hostesses and crew, there is a mad scramble for coats and cases whilst the plane is still taxiing. I suppose it does no harm, but it always reminds me of the Gadarene swine, so as usual, I sat obstinately, still buckled into my seat.

They were certainly right about the cold. There had been a heavy fall of snow and there were long queues outside the terminal for taxis. For some unknown reason, I got one to myself and even better I was lucky enough not to get one of the specialist talkers, so my ignorance of the Mets' and Yankees' doings was not exposed. It was a Sunday evening, but there was still a lot of traffic and as we bowled along the turnpike and left Queens behind, we took the big left-hand bend and I enjoyed the sight of my third favourite American building; a small twenty-storey block with all the grace of Alcatraz with a big neon sign which said, 'Retirement apartments for sale and rent.' This bald statement had always intrigued me because I could not help wondering what kind of American would want to retire to the edge of the Long Island Expressway. Maybe it was for long-distance truck-drivers, growing lonely in their old age.

For a swinging city, New York always seems very quiet on a Sunday evening and even Manhattan seemed deserted as we swung off Lexington and rolled into the covered back

entrance of the Waldorf. Every time I do this I look at the
Barclay and its gallant efforts to look old-fashioned British
and feel something of a traitor, but the finest hot chocolate
in the world always makes the Waldorf win out.

There is a special suite of rooms on the seventeenth floor
for poverty-stricken Englishmen and that is where I landed.
I had had the rooms before and there is a kind of schoolboy
satisfaction with the familiarity and a great feeling of being
a much-travelled man. I switched on the television and listened to it whilst I was shaving. New York City had indulged
in three murders that day and seventeen fires. I was
strongly advised to visit the Van Gogh exhibition at the
Guggenheim, and Mayor Lindsay apparently had a strike
of garbage collectors on his hands. Despite the cold, there
was news of riot trouble in Dallas and L.A., and the big
news from Europe was that a St Bernard dog had got lost
in the snow in Surrey.

I noticed that the little red light on the bedside telephone
was glowing quietly to itself and I checked with the operator who took messages. It seemed that a Mr Railton had
telephoned an hour earlier to say that he would call on me,
and was in fact, now waiting in the lobby and would be
grateful if I would meet him at the Carousel bar.

My trip to New York was for a round of meetings with
Jack Tinker and Partners and the rest of the Interpublic
circus and, no doubt, Mr Railton was their guy who did the
social welcome bit, so I sent him my compliments and the
glad news that I would be down in ten minutes. I proposed
spending the ten minutes downing the first two Waldorf-
type hot chocolates.

When I got to the lobby, I sat at one of the tables at the
edge of the Carousel, and, except for two large men at the
farthest table, reading the *Chicago Daily News* and *Play-
boy* respectively, the place was deserted. Not having the
courage to ask for hot chocolate at a bar, I sipped a rather
fierce John Collins, and after five minutes one of the flun-
keys came over and said that Mr Railton would love to
entertain me in his suite.

The suite was on the 38th floor, and from the look of the

decorations in the hallway it was definitely not the floor for British tourists. The flunkey knocked on the door and a voice with a British accent called out, 'Come in.'

A man in a brown suit got up from a beautiful Bergère couch and came across with hand extended. 'Hello, Edward my boy.'

No possible Mr Railton this man whom I had last seen in London in 1947, in one of those beautifully panelled little set-ups that MI6 finds so necessary to its trade in Queen Anne's Gate. This man's name was actually Bill Righton, a double first at Cambridge, with honours in French and German, but couldn't ask a girl to have a drink with him in either language. When I last saw him, he was trying hard to persuade me to stay on in the racket, and his main line of approach was that a job in civvy street as a draughtsman for £7. 10. 0. a week was a bit of a come-down from colonel's pay. He didn't omit to mention, of course, that MI6 pay was tax free. Like all people who spend a lot of time waffling about King and Country, he was convinced that tax-free dough was the big attraction for everybody else. We had done most of our training to-gether at Winchester and Matlock and knew one another very well, but this meant no more than that we had a guarded respect for each other, certainly no great friend-ship.

Shortly after we had sat down and were verbally walking round one another, the waiter came in and it was typical of the old firm that he was carrying a tray which had on it a bottle of rye and two hot chocolates. I didn't say anything, but I took the point. I guessed that the chit-chat was part of the routine, and I was not going to be told what it was all about without asking; so I asked.

'Jim Railton would like advice on a problem we've got.'

'Does Jim Railton operate in New York then?'

'Oh no, he still operates in London, but we thought it would be better if we had a little chat with you over here.'

'You mean you and James have actually trailed across from London to New York just for a chat?'

It turned out that it might be for rather more than a chat

and it was implied that the journey was considered worth while. I had barely got the words out that I was only too happy to give James Railton advice if he felt I could help after all this time, when he reached for the phone, dialled a number, waited for a few moments, and then hung up without saying a word. Looking rather embarrassed at the secret service touch, he asked me how business was and I gathered that nothing I told him was news. After about five minutes, in walked James Railton, the charm was still there and he didn't look a day older. He was on far too high a level to go in for any ritual dance and he got down to business straight away.

'It's marvellous to see you again, Edward, and I am very grateful that you feel you can help us.'

He pulled a foolscap envelope from his inside pocket and I could see an airline ticket sticking out.

'It's a very simple little matter really, and it will take three days at the very outside.'

'I can't possibly spare one day, let alone three. I've got meetings tomorrow morning and for the rest of the week, so there's no room for any days off.'

'Of course, of course,' he said. 'Now I hope you'll forgive me but I know some of the Interpublic people very well and they will be only too happy to rearrange all the meetings absolutely to your convenience.'

'That's great for Interpublic, but I don't work for them and my own lot aren't going to be too happy at me swanning around the States for several days at their expense.'

'Who said anything about swanning around the States for several days.'

'The airline ticket in the envelope.'

James smiled. 'Well, we've got a little consolation prize for you which I'm sure would have happened anyway. I gather you've been after the Cunard account recently. They mentioned it to me at the Travellers' Club only a couple of weeks ago and I have a letter from them here for you. I understand the account is yours from the first of next month.'

I was pleased as a dog with two tails, but at the same

time I realized that with this kind of string pulling, they must have been setting operations up for at least two months and I didn't like the sound of that at all.

'Well, what we would like you to do is pop down to Dallas tomorrow with one of our American friends and just have a look at the passengers coming in on an internal flight from San Antonio. See if there's anybody you recognize and that's it.'

I looked over at him and grinned. 'You know, James, you remind me of my grandma.'

'Well, that's very nice, Edward, because I seem to remember you were rather fond of your grandma, but I'm a little lost as to where the resemblance lies.'

'Well, when my grandma was going to the shops, she always said, "I suppose I shall have to trail to the shops" and when I had to go to the shops, it was always, "I would like you to pop to the shops", and bearing in mind that Dallas is the thick end of another three thousand miles, it works out that I'll be doing a cosy round trip of six thousand miles just to look at some passengers getting off a plane. Anyway, who's the American friend? Do I know him?'

'No, you don't know him, but he's very experienced, worked in SOE and is now with the CIA. His name's Bill Autenowski; a very reliable man. As a matter of fact, I've asked him to drop in later to have a drink with you and Bill.'

He reached out and handed me the envelope which, without examining too carefully, I could see contained an air ticket and a very thick wad of hundred-dollar notes; all nice and dirty and genuine-looking. He stood up and said, 'Perhaps you would like to stroll down and see me off the premises.'

We walked through the lobby, and whilst the doorman was looking out for a cab, he put his arm on mine and said, without his official voice, 'I was so sorry to hear about Sally,' and even after all those years, I found it too sad to be able to answer. He patted me on the shoulder and went out to join the doorman on Park Avenue. I went back to the suite on the 38th floor. American elevators are very fast and very smooth and I suppose it must have taken about forty seconds from when I pressed the button till it arrived at the 38th. I felt very lonely because I saw her again, the long blonde hair streaming out in the wind, she had her arms out wide and she was running towards me. A bit like a foal, but foals don't have big soft mouths like poppies and they don't say 'Sweetie, you're early'. I wondered if I would be more lonely or less lonely if I knew where she was buried.

The man with Bill Righton was big and ugly and attractive and the massive friendly hand and the big smile and the 'Hi Ted, how you doin'' did me a lot of good. I don't care whether Americans are sincere or not, I lap it up and like it. We chatted about mutual friends and then I said to Bill Autenowski, 'Where do we meet tomorrow?'

'I'll call at your room at seven.'

I knew it was naughty but why the hell not, so I said: 'Am I looking for a man or a woman tomorrow or don't we know.'

Autenowski looked at Bill Righton, who adjusted his spectacles and smiled his mysterious smile.

'We're not trying to make things hard, Ted, but it's better if you don't know.'

CHAPTER ELEVEN

When we got out of the plane at Dallas the heat rocked me, I'd never been in Texas before and the thermostat must have been set for roasting. It was like standing in a furnace. Bill Autenowski obviously carried weight because there was no palaver and in five minutes we were in a room with air conditioning and mirrors you could see through. On a table there were two pairs of binoculars and a Nikon with a long lens and drinks and all that. Bill looked at his watch and smiled. 'There's been a delay at San Antonio so they won't be here for an hour and a half yet.'

He eased his massive frame back, not for comfort but as a kind of sign of discomfort and he looked at me. 'This thing's kinda important to us, Ted, so I really don't go along with some of this crap – we're looking for a guy – at least you are.'

'Who is he?'

He shrugged. 'I'm not in on that, I don't know a thing except they think you may recognize a certain guy and the word is, he's on the flight from San Antonio.'

The phone rang about two hours later and Bill listened, said 'O.K., thanks' and hung up and looked over at me.

'The flight's arrived, they'll be coming through in ten minutes and they're going to keep 'em slowed down as they go by.'

And eleven minutes later they started coming through. I didn't use the binoculars, they weren't really necessary and I could easily miss someone in the small field of view. We had been given a passenger list and there were no names I recognized out of the passengers, men or women. There were thirty-four passengers and five crew. They all passed the ticket desk slowly and I didn't recognize a soul and the passengers were being assembled by an air hostess, I saw a tall man yawn and slowly fall to the ground and I heard Bill gasp. I said, 'The fellow's fainted or something,' and

Bill said, 'Oh the stupid, stupid bastards.'

He put down the binoculars and sat down. After a few moments he looked up at me and said, 'I'll have to take you to the morgue for you to see that guy close up.'

'Never seen him in my life, Bill.'

'We'll have to go through the drill all the same.'

There's not much you can say for morgues, except that in Dallas they're beautifully cool. They turned back the sheet and I looked at a thin drawn face a bit like an Indian's. They had stitched the eyelids open so that I could see his eyes and Bill insisted that the whole sheet come off. There was a man standing around who looked like a cop in plain clothes and he called Bill 'sir'.

'He's been checked by the steward, the captain and two passengers who we know.'

I asked, 'Checked for what?'

The cop looked at Bill who nodded.

'Checked that he was the guy who was shot at the airport – no question of mixed up cadavers.'

And that was the first time I noticed the wound. Death must have been instantaneous, it was right through his heart, and now they'd patched him up it was hardly visible.

'I didn't even hear a shot,' and Bill said, 'You wouldn't Ted – anyway they used a silencer.'

I looked at him. 'How the hell do you know they used a silencer, we couldn't hear anyway.'

He looked uncomfortable. 'Don't worry, Ted, I just do.'

'Do you want me to look at the other passengers.'

He shrugged. 'No, this was the guy.'

'You said you didn't know who it was.'

Bill nodded to the cop and said, 'Thanks, Joe,' and the big hand took my arm and said, 'We'll go down-town and have a drink, Ted, and talk.'

I always have to work out what down-town means to Americans – it just doesn't sound like the posh bit but it is. Between two second-hand car places there was a building without windows, not very big but very plain. I would have guessed it was a small furniture depository and I would have been wrong. A hand-painted notice said: 'The Captain's Bar – good drink and Go-Go girls.' Bill was obviously known and he led me expertly in the dim light to a table for two. The music was loud and the Go-Go girl was in a sort of bamboo cage. I could see no obvious reason for the cage, the drinkers were talking not looking, so it wasn't to keep them out, and the girl in the cage epitomized the girl next door – plain, thin, tatty and bored, she waggled inexpertly about every fifth beat and I doubt if she could have walked out unaided.

Bill leaned back in his chair and it only just took the strain; the drinks came, he took a good swig of his bourbon and leaned over, arms on the table, and the huge shoulders looked like Grand Central Station. He looked at me for a few seconds as if deciding whether I was ready for the good news. He voted for 'yes', and said, 'Ted, the guy back there was a KGB guy so we won't shed any tears about him. The set-up was that maybe you'd identify him. Your lot and my lot are looking for a guy whose name is Berger and the records say you know him. We knew he was one of three guys but we didn't know which because they all have cover names. What else we know is that Berger is highly valued by the KGB. The plan was that after he'd been identified by you we could really concentrate on the one guy. We know that Berger is doing something big – but we've no idea what it is. We had a joint British–American meeting and my lot were all for knocking off all three. The British said no, on the grounds that we need to know what this guy Berger is up to before he's knocked off.'

He wound his glass around on the table. 'Looks to me like the CIA have done it their way. I'll need to check up if they've knocked off the other two suspects as well. We're staying at the Hilton tonight, and when I've done my checking I'll come back to you.'

The Berger bit made sense of a lot of things that had seemed odd from the past, and it ironed out a lot of the creases, but I had a feeling it was shouting something else to me but I couldn't grasp what it was. We were soon installed at the Hilton and Bill went off to whatever bushes the CIA use for meetings in Dallas. I've stayed in Hiltons all over the world and, despite what people say, I like them. I think in a way they strengthen my belief in natural justice with a large dash of sex thrown in.

The sex and the justice are both shaped like Liz Taylor. If there wasn't such a thing as natural justice how does a craggy-looking working-class Welshman end up with a dish like that when she could have had every Hilton in the world like she was playing Monopoly.

My sense of justice generally generates thirst and hunger, so I had a few drinks and then went to Trader Vic's and was discussing the virtues of Dimple Haig with the barman when Bill loomed up beside us like the *Ark Royal* and said quietly, with renewed faith in the U.S. Intelligence system, 'The other two guys are O.K. Let's go to my room.'

It seemed that it wasn't a rift between Washington and London, it was Texans waving the old flag of independence again. If there were KGB guys trotting through Texas, then to hell with Washington, Foggy Bottom, London and St James; they were going to get plugged, and good. The two suspects who were left still alive and well, one working at the U.N. as a clerk and the other in London – and he worked in finance or exports or something in the City. We both put our silver dollars on the clerk at the U.N.

CHAPTER TWELVE

We both lost our silver dollars on the clerk at the United Nations, he wasn't old enough by ten years to have been Berger. And not all the best Moscow surgery would have turned Berger's craggy face into the soft pale moon worn by the CIA suspect.

Bill and I flew back to London that day and all the lights of London were laid out like pearl necklaces and rubies as we circled for fifteen minutes in the 'box' over Heathrow.

We had a meeting next morning in the 'safe house' in Ebury Street. There was a thin Special Branch file and a slightly thicker MI5 file on the third man. They both had photographs and they were both Berger. He'd aged better than I had, but according to his dossier he wasn't married and maybe that's what made the difference. There were record cards from his dentist and doctor and I smiled to see that he had an appendix scar. He ran the traditional KGB type of business – import/export of a wide variety of goods – but he didn't trade with any of the Iron Curtain countries, mainly the United States and Latin America. His goods ranged from toys through stationery to something called computer peripherals, which turned out to be the bits and pieces you hang on and plug into computers. No convictions, but one driving licence endorsement for crossing a red light. No close friends, male or female, but he used two girls, expensive call girls – but not in tandem. He lived in Putney in a block of flats and the only noted peculiarity was that he sometimes said 'Hello' to other occupants; it was put down to his being a foreigner. He had three passports that had been traced – U.S.A., British and Canadian. None had visas for any communist country.

The company was a limited company with issued capital of £2,000, and he had three bank accounts adding up to an average of £70,000 each. He had reported three break-ins at his flat to the local police. Two were genuine and one was a botched job by Special Branch. They had taken his camera and some rolls of exposed film. He hadn't mentioned this to the police, but when the Special Branch photographic section developed the films they were quite innocent. That is, if you count full frontal nudes of very pretty blondes as innocent.

*   *   *

Jim Railton stuck his head round the door and said, 'If you're ready we'll go to the other office and have a meeting.'

The other office was in the Passport Office building in Petty France. And there was Joe Steiner, with grey hair that was almost white and four younger men in their thirties who I didn't know. James Railton sat at the head of the table and, without any preliminaries, he leaned forward towards me and the gentle brown eyes looked at me steadily.

'Ted, you're probably not going to like what I have to say but it's got to be said so I'd better get on with it. We want you to work for us – it could take four or five months and it certainly will not take longer than a year.'

'Do you mean full-time?'

No hesitation, 'Yes.'

'What about my job?'

He half smiled. 'That's about the only nice bit I've got to say. We have spoken to your people and when it's finished you'll get a seat on the board and twenty per cent of the equity. You'll get a guaranteed tax-free payment from us for a year at £4,000 a month plus all expenses and even if it finishes before a year the payout will continue for a year. So you'll end up with about £50,000 capital and a stake in your agency paid for by us.'

'And what if I refuse?'

The brown eyes were too honest to look away but he did have the decency to sigh, 'You won't get your job back and you won't get another.'

I was staggered. 'But, James, that's just plain blackmail – you can't do this.'

A few moments' silence. 'Yes, Ted, it is – but we can do it – we just don't want to.'

'But why can't someone else do the job – if it's to do with Berger I've already fingered him for you. Let someone else take over.'

'There are two reasons why it has to be you, Ted – one I can tell you and one I can't. The one I can tell you is that we know too little about what Berger is up to and there's a chance that something from way back could give you a clue. You're the only one who's had anything to do with him ever.'

'How do you know it's all that important.'

'We do, Ted, leave it at that – Berger's been left here quietly by the KGB for fifteen years and he's paying off now, and it must be a big pay off for an investment like that.'

'And what's the reason that you can't tell me?'

'I can't tell you, Ted, and that's final, but if you knew you'd say yes to my proposition right now.'

I looked around the table but everyone was looking at papers or making notes. Only Joe Steiner had the decency to look over at me, but he didn't speak.

'Can I phone my office?'

'Sure.'

I dialled and asked for the chairman – he was not available, two other directors were not available, my secretary had given notice the day before. I got the message. There was not much to think about really. I had the flat in the King's Road, the boat at Marlow, my books and my job, or had had my job. No ties, no one to persuade – in fact no one who even cared. I suddenly realized how little reason I had to be alive.

I didn't thank them for bringing me to this bit of self-realization, but I knew it was true and I knew that they'd worked it out months ago when I still thought I belonged in the world. I knew I'd never got over Sally and Sammy, and down at bedrock I was just passing the time till I died and it didn't matter much how I passed it. It was a piece of careful cruelty and I wondered how many hours had been spent working it all out. I went back to the seat at the table and looked down at the two dossiers, not that I could see them because my eyes were blurred and a tear splashed down on a buff cover and it sounded like an explosion. The noise of the traffic outside was faint, but it was part of a sane world, an ordinary world. Without looking up I said, 'O.K., James, we'd better get on with it.' And he said quietly, 'Ted, it may end better than you think right now – and I mean that.'

I looked up at him. 'I'm 48, far too old for this sort of caper and you must know it, but if you and Joe will go to these lengths then I can only hope you're right, but you must be bloody thin on the ground when you need to press-gang middle-aged men.'

James half smiled. 'A fair analogy in the circumstances, Ted, but a wrong assumption; we want you back because we need you, we need your thinking like we needed it back in the war, and if it's any consolation your agency raised merry hell because they need you too.'

'Christ, it sounds like Pontius Pilate, the Sanhedrin and Barabbas.'

Joe Steiner smiled at long last. 'You're feeling better, Ted, you're getting nasty.'

He looked at James Railton who nodded, and Joe said, 'Let me give you the general picture, Ted. Sort of bring you up-to-date. There's very little of our budget spent on 1 (a) now – stuff like weapons, intentions, troops and movements. With satellites and electronics and just reading the technical Press, we've got a pretty good picture that's updated almost to thirty minutes lapsed time. There are areas of concern to us, like germ-warfare, pollution and secret weapons – small ones not big ones, political intentions and so on. Most of our time and money gets spent on what's going on in the U.S.S.R. inside – industrially, politically and economically. Militarily the two sides are so well balanced and the counter-measures, and counter-counters go on and on so that in our assessment there's not a cat in hell's chance of a war between the U.S.A. and the U.S.S.R.' He smiled wearily. 'In fact, we're spending quite a bit of dough exercising our minds on how Europe comes out when the two big boys become allies. China's a hot potato and neither side is going to hold it or try to – they've both had bloody noses for just touching it, let alone holding, and in our present problem it's a very safe assumption that Berger is working solely in the U.K. and solely for the U.S.S.R. In the early days they used him for some odd-ball things, but whenever he came under any surveillance he was pulled out fast. But for three months now he's had four KGB guys over either working for him or protecting him or both. There's a full dossier, photographs and film of all of them available for you in the Central Intelligence Room, and his set-up is definitely operative; there's just a smell coming out of his outfit that says this is the pay-off time. He's definitely back in our business.'

'What area is he operating in?'

Joe leaned back, 'We haven't a clue – and I mean that literally – it's all hunch and guess and instinct.'

He waved a hand at the unknowns round the table, 'These fellows will fill you in on their special areas and from then on it's all yours – you can have any help you want, and although we don't expect any rough stuff we've laid on a weapons and up-to-date self-defence course for you. But I'd rather you heard these young fellows first.'

James Railton broke in, looking at his watch, 'Look, we'll be back at two-thirty. Bill, Joe, Ted and I are lunching at the Travellers and I've booked a table and we're already late.'

While we were having a pre-lunch drink James walked me over to one of the big windows and said, 'Just in case you get any wrong ideas about democracy, Ted, I think I ought to tell you that we had to go to both the Foreign Secretary and the Home Secretary before we were given permission to pressure you, and I can assure you that we didn't get an easy ride – neither of them liked the whole idea; they put their reasons across in no uncertain terms and they both have insisted on being kept informed on a weekly basis.'

After lunch I felt worn out and I asked if the specialist

briefings could be held over to the next day. This was agreed to and Bill Autenowski helped me collect my bags together and we got a taxi back to the flat at King's Road. Bill was younger than me, but because of sheer size and character he was a tonic. We treated ourselves to a Glenfiddich and looked out of the long windows down Royal Avenue. The supermarket was crowded with nice ordinary people who had no inkling of what was done in their name and in their interests, and who wouldn't have believed half of it if they had been told. It was April and the minis were out and the girls looked gentle and far away from our kind of stupidities.

The flat had two bedrooms and a large lounge, and the large lounge had three walls covered with books, mainly Penguins, and Bill looked them over, head on one side as he read the titles on the spines. They say you can tell a lot about a man by checking his book shelves, but all you would have got from mine was an impression of a man who didn't know what he wanted to know but was trying hard to find out. And that, I guess, wouldn't have been too inaccurate an assessment. By the side of my bed was the Penguin version of Montaigne's Essays and Palgrave and a copy of John Clare's poems. If you spend a long time being sad you need to read old things, things that comment on the common denominators of life throughout man's history. There's a terrible need for perspective when you're sad, because you feel like a smudge on the road, caught in a car's headlights, that an hour before was a hedgehog on his way to a meal.

I had a bath, introduced Bill to Glazunov's Violin Concerto, and Pierre Fournier playing Tchaikovsky's 'Variations on a Rococo Theme'. Musically, I suppose they're about the same level as 'Moon River' and 'Gigi', but they last half an hour longer. I knew that when he'd gone I'd play Mendelssohn's fiddle concerto, but it had a big scrawl on the sleeve, 'Dearest sweetie, this is how I feel about you – Sally.' There was a gold ring somewhere about from Lara inscribed, 'Je t'aime infiniment' – a more elaborate effort but I knew which message was true. Why are phonies always so much better at being phonies than genuine lovers are at telling their love. And suddenly my bells rang and I turned to Bill.

'Bill, for Christ's sake how do I get hold of James Railton?'

He put his drink down. 'I'll get him for you.'

He dialled. 'Jim – Ted wants you.' He turned to me. 'Do you want to speak to him or shall he come round?'

'Would he mind coming round and Joe Steiner.'

He spoke for a few moments, hung up and said, 'They'll be around in about twenty minutes – if you dial RAILTON you'll get James any time.' He was professional and patient, he didn't ask what I wanted and, riffling through my records, he put on an LP of Eddie Duchin playing 'Manhattan' – we both liked it and by the time we'd played it four times there was a ring at the doorbell.

'I'll let them in.' His foot was against the bottom of the door quite automatically but it was our own dear boys. James in a dinner jacket and Joe Steiner in slacks and lumberjack shirt.

They sat themselves down uninvited.

'Joe, I'd like to go back to when I first knew Berger.'

'O.K., but he wasn't part of my responsibility then, it was you and David Law if I remember rightly.'

'Yes, but you took over the network.'

'Sure, but I folded it up pretty damn quick.'

'But they told me they'd caught Otto Sander, the German Abwehr operator and they hadn't.'

'O.K.'

'And they knew your name, David Law's name and my name.'

'I guess that was about it.'

'Was there ever any indication that they knew more.'

'No – I'm sure,' said Joe, 'that was all they knew.'

'Right – Otto Sander had been in the next cell to Berger in the gaol at Hildesheim.'

'O.K.'

'And I put them both there.'

'O.K.'

68

'Nothing to connect them and me to you and David,' I went on.

'That figures.'

'There was an absolute cut-off round my operation except for the DDMI and the Foreign Office?'

Joe nodded.

'So you could expect the NKVD to have heard of you two but not of my actual operation.'

'Why not your operation?'

'Because it was a seconded operation to the Foreign Office.'

'Go on.'

'So someone at the Foreign Office knew the bottom bit – my operation, but not only that, he knew about you and David which was not his to know.'

Joe smiled. 'And you're suggesting the DDMI tipped off the NKVD.'

'No.'

'Well, are you suggesting that James and I did?'

'No.'

'Well, for Christ sake get to the point them.'

'Who was in charge of the MI6 liaison at the Foreign Office at that time?'

'God knows.'

'Can you check.'

'Right now?'

I nodded. Joe looked so like Spencer Tracy as he pursed his lips and went to the phone and dialled. He was there for about ten minutes. When he came back he said, 'You've got a bull's eye there, boy, but I don't know what the hell it means – Kim Philby was in charge at that time.' And then it all fitted in.

'That's why Berger was so desperate not to go in the nick for a month or so – he was working for the NKVD then. They meant to put him on the Americans but he got demobbed so they stuck him on us. That's how the Russians knew about you and David and me from Philby, and Otto Sander from Berger, and Philby had to give them the two ends of the story but no middle – they hadn't a clue what we were doing – just some names.' James Railton, who hadn't spoke up to then, said quickly, 'What made you think of this now, Ted?'

I stopped to think and I couldn't. How the hell do you explain how you think.

'I don't know, James, I was thinking about a lot of other things nothing to do with this and it just came into my mind.'

Joe shook his head. 'A bloody queer way to work, Ted, but it seems to work; but I don't see how it helps us right now.'

'If Berger was working for Philby then maybe he's working for him now.'

Joe looked up. 'Now that's a bright thought, my boy, so what the hell is Philby doing now.'

I showed surprise. 'Can't you find out, Joe?'

He grinned, 'Sure I can but not on this damn phone. I'll see you tomorrow, but it may take longer – I'll let you know.'

It did take longer. The next day I spent down in the basement of St Alphage House on the firing range of the Marylebone Pistol Club where a guy from the Special Branch worked on me for hours on the 25-metre range with an automatic ·22. By mid-afternoon the clusters of fifteen were getting closer and closer together and he was satisfied. They had chosen a Browning 9 mm for me, and we practised loading and unloading and then we stripped it down. The next day I had a felt holster that fitted neatly under my left armpit and we both knew that provided the other guy wasn't too good and missed with his first two shots, I'd survive.

At the Duke of Wellington Barracks in Chelsea we went through the unarmed combat bit all over again. There was nothing very new, and, like riding a bicycle, it's an art you don't forget, and the police sergeant who tried me out wasn't used to pupils who did it back like they meant it. Once you've done it that way you're stuck with it, which is bloody inconvenient in civilian life because it means if you get in a fight the other guy generally gets a broken neck instead of two loose teeth. I felt there was just a touch of spite when the sergeant said, 'Maybe we'd better cut down on our smoking a bit, sir.'

So I kept a straight face and said, 'Well, let's go and get that thumb of yours properly set before the MO clocks off.'

It was three days before Bill and I met James and Joe again. Joe looked puzzled, 'Well, Ted, Philby's bank account gets filled from the KGB coffers, they're not doing him too badly either, but he seems to be spending all his time on work for various trade missions and delegations.'

'Missions in general?'

'General in terms of what they cover but particular in as much as they are only those to this country – there's a couple of Yanks doing the U.S.A. but they don't spend as much time on their missions as Philby does on ours.'

'What missions do they send here.'

'Well, I've laid on young Maclean, one of the lads at the meeting the other day, to give us a special briefing if you want it.'

'When.'

'You say, boy, and you get.'

'Let's have him round now.'

Joe stood up. 'We'll go round to Petty France, Ted; it's safer there. By the way, your phone's tapped and recorded, Special Branch are tailing you and keeping an eye on this place and just to round things off there's at least three bugging devices spread around your little nest, you might find one but two you won't find.'

'Thanks, Joe – when did you do it.'

'While you were in New York.' He grinned and slapped my back. 'All good clean fun, my boy, we've got to take care of our investment.'

CHAPTER THIRTEEN

Jock Maclean was about thirty-five, crew-cut hair, rimless glasses and not given to smiling, but he had the dope on Russian missions in files that were feet high and half covering the table. He waited for someone to give him the off and James said, 'O.K. Jock, you just give us the general picture.'

'Well, gentleman, I've compiled all Eastern Bloc missions into one file and they cover two types of inquiries that they make – consumer goods and capital goods. In consumer goods there are a few things they genuinely want to buy but not much. In this area they're really after visits to factories for know-how and straight copying. If we care we lead them up the garden path from time to time but we don't care all that much – they've got good know-how in most things. But in heavy engineering they are generally looking for real – they want turn-key operations. We put together a consortium and provide the whole shooting match. We choose their site and build them a rolling mill complete, and hand it over with project leaders to get started. This is mainly big stuff – heavy engineering, tyre factories, car plants, steel mills and the like. We've been doing quite well out of it and there's good co-operation on both sides.'

I interrupted. 'How do we get paid.'

'Gold, dollars and a lot of barter – wheat and leather and so on.'

'What's our most recent big order from them.'

'An ICL computer installation worth three million for a car plant.'

'With peripherals?'

He looked up amazed. 'Do you know about computers then, sir?'

'No.'

'Why the question about peripherals?'

'What's the answer, Jock?'

'No, we don't get much from peripherals because they do excellent peripherals themselves in East Germany.'

'What are they looking at at the moment?'

He hesitated. 'Well, that's an odd point, sir, because over the last two months they've drawn back from most of the deals they were negotiating or talking about.'

'What kind of deals?'

'Oh a wide range, sir, a ball-bearing plant, a bakery plant, a stripmill, a foundry and all computer software.'

'Software – what's that, the paper it gets printed on.'

He smiled. 'No, sir, its a bit of jargon, it's really the thinking – the programming and design of systems for use on computers.'

'Any idea why?'

'They said it was a question of waiting for the next five-year plan, but that's pretty unlikely because five-year plans are only political announcements – a sort of election campaign – they don't work to them in practice.'

We chatted away for another hour or so and then called it a day.

'One final question, Jock. Does this drawing back affect our trade balance much?'

'No, not really, all these things are in high demand by all the under-developed countries – it's consumer goods that affect us more in the export field.'

Nobody seemed to have anything more to ask him so he bowed out and left us to our own thoughts.

Joe Steiner looked sceptical. 'I can't see a high grade KGB guy like Berger being used on anything to do with trade missions, can you, Ted?'

'Not really, but there may be a clue there somewhere and if the KGB are being used for industrial espionage maybe he's the clearing house.'

Joe looked disgusted. 'Aw, Ted, come off it, you can use any dumb-bell for that or alternatively a guy who knows a hell of a lot about high technology industry, and that chap's a plain god-damn spy. One of their hundred damn attachés could do it better.'

73

'Joe, is there much clandestine radio traffic from the U.K.?'

'Don't know, son, but Signals can soon tell us.' He lifted the phone without any great enthusiasm, 'nine four'. He put his hand over the phone. 'This thing's a bloody marvel – I say the number and some bloody electronic thing has to recognize my voice pattern before I get a reply – they told me my pattern's almost the same as Louis Armstrong.' After a few minutes he lifted his head. 'Martin, Steiner here. Have you had much clandestine radio traffic over the last two months or so?' He listened intently. 'O.K., what's that mean to a guy like me – well why hasn't somebody found out? ... Well do it for God's sake – you guys need a bloody nanny!' He bashed down the phone. 'No excessive traffic but they've had bursts of alternated high-speed high frequency oscillations whatever that means, and they don't know what it is. They're playing the tapes slow and fast and have put cyphers on to it but got no sense out of it so far – sounds to me like it could be something.'

CHAPTER FOURTEEN

I decided to go down to the boat at Marlow for a couple of days. I've a Fjord Ambassador with twin Volvos, accommodation for six and it was a beautiful quiet mooring at Temple Lock. There are wild violets, orchids and 'fraises des bois' on the banks, and you almost have to boot the squirrels and rabbits out of the way because they see so few human beings. There's my own small jetty with plug-in mains electricity and plug-in telephone, which doesn't often get plugged in. *Samantha* was lying there calm and easy, just moving gently with the current of the Thames as it flowed towards the weir. The cockpit was dry as a bone and there was almost no water in the bilges. I neglected her disgracefully but she was always smiling and welcoming when I arrived. I turned the keys on the control panel and the Volvos came to life as if they had been used an hour before – no hesitation. Some boats are like devils and some are like angels, and *Samantha* was an angel. I slackened the warps a little and walked around the deck; it was great to feel the movement of a boat under my feet. This boat was all woman, or a man's idea of woman anyway – responsive, forgiving, flattering and relaxing; no matter what wind or tide, she came into moorings gently and easily.

I was checking over the instruments and had just switched on the echo-sounder when the phone rang. Which was impossible because it wasn't plugged in. I went down the steps to the main cabin and there it was, the flex was coiled round it and it wasn't plugged in. It kept ringing and finally I lifted the receiver but I didn't say anything, but straightaway a voice said, 'Is that Hurley 461.' That's my number but I still didn't speak. Then the voice said again, 'Is that Hurley 461, I have a call for you.'

'Who is calling?'

'Mr Steiner.' And there was a click and sure enough it was Joe on the other end.

'Joe, my phone isn't plugged in at the jetty – it just isn't connected to anything.'

There was a laugh. 'Don't worry, fella, all part of modern science. I think it's called a remote activator – they must have fitted it just in case.' It was going to take me time to get used to being back in the business.

'What can I do for you, Joe?'

'Oh nothing, just relax, we just wanted to know you were down there – call me or James if you want anything. By the way, we've opened an account for you in Zurich and the first month's pay is already deposited. There's some cash in fivers in the chain locker in your for'ard cabin. Don't get lonely,' and he hung up.

There was £300 in the chain locker in a canvas bag. I've always found that the best way of sorting out a problem is to ignore it for at least a whole day, so the next day I spent oiling hinges, testing pumps and took *Samantha* up to Harleyford and then down to the Compleat Angler at Marlow and had a good meal. The next morning I phoned James and asked for a list of all our suspect Berger's customers and a list of all the companies visited by U.S.S.R. trade missions and a current appraisal of their interest. About three hours later a white Mini appeared through the trees and a Field Security sergeant got out and walked over and saluted.

'Documents for you, sir.'

I looked up at him conscious of my dirty slacks and sweaty shirt. 'How do you know they are for me?'

He smiled, he was just a boy, but enthusiastic, and he pulled out an envelope, and when I pulled out the contents there was a diagram showing my mooring, an up-to-date photograph of me and a separate photograph of *Samantha* and his own identity card. I handed them back to him and asked him if he'd like a cup of tea but he blushed and said, 'I'd better be getting back, sir, there's a bit of a panic on.'

'What about.'

The blue eyes were young but they were very alert. 'I gather you know more about that than I do, sir.'

I nodded and he saluted again and went off. They hadn't

given me an impression of a panic, it had all seemed very calm, but I guess that there was a lot being done that I didn't know about. I undid the parcel and it was pages of names and addresses and a long report on trade missions – and a hand-written note from Joe which said, 'In case you didn't know, our friend has a boat at Temple Island, just below Henley, he owns the island. The boat is a forty-foot Meakes "Sea Lion" class – twin Volvos. He never takes it out – just uses it as a gin palace for business entertaining. Goes pretty regularly at week-ends.'

I decided to have a look around the boat that night. I knew Temple Island but had never been on it, and from the chart it looked about 300 yards long by about 100 wide.

CHAPTER FIFTEEN

The locks on the River Thames close at eight on summer evenings, and as I slipped through the lock at Hurley I decided to go up-river to Henley, which would give me an opportunity of looking at Temple Island and then if it were necessary on the return journey I could come in with the engines cut, with the flow of the river. I stayed talking with the lock-keeper at Hurley until it was five past eight, which meant that no boats would be moving through Hurley Lock or Marsh Lock, up-stream from Henley, until the next morning.

As I went past Temple Island it was much as I remembered. Some horse-chestnuts, a few Lombardy poplars and a little Palladian folly which looked as if it had been converted into some sort of living quarters as there were chintz curtains at the windows. The forty-foot 'Sea Lion' was alongside a short jetty and the warps were tied to the bollards with rolls of standard Thames Knots which indicated that she was unlikely to be used at short notice. The curtains were drawn at the cabin windows and portholes, but the flying-deck was clearly visible and it appeared to be crammed full of sea-going instruments and there was a radar quadrant on the roof.

Twenty minutes later I was at Henley where I filled up with petrol and water at Hobb's Boatyard; cruised round both sides of the eyot and checked that there were no vessels moving. Everyone seemed settled down for the night with the exception of one twenty-three-foot Freeman, and the confetti that lay on the deck indicated that bedtime might be later there than for the rest of the river. I cruised up to the weir at Marsh Lock but again there was nothing moving.

There was an hour at least before sundown and I moored on the riverbank with two irons, and indulged in a large tin of baked beans and two éclairs from the Vienna Coffee

Shop in Marlow.

As soon as it was dark I took out the mooring irons, pulled in the warps and nosed *Samantha* out from the bank. When I was down-river from the eyot, in the main-stream, I cut the engines and tried out the drifting conditions. Even after a mile she was still doing two knots, so I lashed a bucket to some nylon rope with which I took a double turn round the ensign standard then threw the bucket over the stern as a sea-anchor. Within seconds we were down to one knot. By now it was almost completely dark, but I could just see the white shape of the pretty little Palladian folly. I steered her round the other side of the island and, with the help of the boathook and an elderberry tree, I nosed her into the soft clay of the bank. With the stern warp in hand I slid into the water, and in a few strokes I was on the bank. I brought her stern round and tied her lightly to a small silver birch. I decided to reconnoitre the folly first and five minutes later I was outside it. There were no lights inside, no sounds and no sign of movement. It had a standard Yale lock and, with the aid of my credit card, it gently opened.

I moved my hand in the dark up the left-hand wall and there was a switch, and I was tempted to use it. I closed the door gently behind me and decided to stick to my torch. Inside, it was just one large room with a double divan in an alcove. On the wall was a Casa Pupo type carpet and the furniture was Swedish neutral, all chrome and teak. There was an office-type desk against the right-hand wall. I was wearing a pair of rubber gloves; the type that housewives use for washing up. They were a bad fit but they avoided fingerprints, and Joe Steiner had warned me that one of the new miracles of modern science was the ability to identify glove prints; but apparently this didn't apply to rubber gloves. I moved over to the desk and went through all the drawers.

The contents were merely household accounts, correspondence with the boatyard concerning the boat and some visiting cards in the name of Louis Barrault, which was Berger's cover name. Several drawers were empty and one contained only a paperback copy of Solzhenitsyn's *The First Circle* which I felt must have made nostalgic reading for a KGB man, a touch of 'Home Sweet Home'.

On the top of the desk was a small note-pad by the telephone. I shone the torch obliquely on the top page and there was a faint impression from some pencil notes. I ripped off the page and put it in my pocket.

There was a cabinet, well filled with booze, and to my surprise a packet of Belyeitzin cigarettes, a bit careless for Berger, but a full search of the room revealed nothing else of interest. As I closed the door of the folly behind me the telephone rang inside. It rang only three times, so the caller was obviously not on urgent business. I stood in the shadow of the tiny 'porte cochère' and looked at Berger's boat. It was warped tight and I could hear the fenders squeaking against the jetty. Across the far bank of the river I could see very dimly the white shape of a small upturned dinghy.

It took a pair of hollow-nosed pliers to open the main saloon door, and a bit of fiddling with a skeleton key, but the boat was obviously well looked after. The door opened and closed without a sound. That was my fourth mistake since landing on the island. I knew the layout of the 'Sea Lion' of old and this was a beautiful specimen but quite standard. There was a ship-to-shore radio-telephone, Pye radar scanner, a Sestrel compass, a Seafarer echo-sounder and all the usual minor instruments. Nothing extraordinary and nothing more than you would need for a cross-Channel journey.

The cabins had the usual collection of sleeping bags and ship's paraphernalia. There was a rather nice touch provided by a silk Red Ensign and a pennant of the Little Ship Club. In the main saloon I lifted back the carpet and the hatch came up easily. The steel staircase went down almost vertically into the engine room. 'Sea Lions' were normally fitted with very large Perkins set to port and starboard of a teak cat-walk. Berger obviously cared about the boat because both engines were housed behind green-painted aluminium venting louvres. When you came to the end of the engines you had to get down on hands and knees, and as I shone the torch I noticed a massive array of batteries. There were ten, two pairs of two had cables leading normally into the diesels, but six were linked in series and the cable wound round the bulkhead and then disappeared into the port engine chamber right at the top. I tried moving the propeller shaft of the starboard engine but it was obvious that it was going to take more horsepower than I could muster, but when I tried the port shaft it turned easily – and then I half guessed what I was going to find. I tried the thin Bowie knife on the screw-heads and finally had to settle for using a penny.

Four screws and six butterfly nuts later and I eased the engine housing away. You didn't need to be a radio expert to know that all that beautiful grey-painted metal-work and the meters and knobs were probably the most advanced piece of radio transmitting and receiving equipment this side of Berlin. Even the Voice of America wouldn't have turned up its nose at this lot. I didn't know enough about radio equipment to make notes so I pushed the housing back and started tightening up the nuts. There was a soft precision thud as it went into place, and an echoing thud which seemed to come from the hull, and not noticing that, was mistake number five.

I checked back to where a telescopic, hydraulic aerial was situated and there was in fact a cluster of five. The boys in Signals Security would have great fun with this little lot, but I had a kind of feeling that it was time to go.

I had gone up the steel ladder, had gently let down the hatch-cover and pulled back the saloon carpet before I noticed the man sitting on the starboard navigator's seat. He had a crew-cut but he was not an American. I had already seen his face on film and slides in the Central Intelligence Room. There had been film of him feeding the ducks in St Jame's Park – with the assistance of the Third Secretary from the Russian Embassy. Slides of him getting out of a taxi, eating an ice-cream at Battersea Fun Fair and sitting on a park bench in Kensington Gardens.

His name was Kowalski and I doubt if even his mother

would have loved him if she could have seen him now. He had a scar down his right cheek and he was so still I couldn't even see him breathing – but if anybody wasn't breathing it was me.

The five mistakes registered in my mind in approximately one second. Mistake number one was not doing a recce of the island right at the start. Mistake number two was not recognizing that the telephone ringing was a signal. Mistake number three was not recognizing that the white dinghy on the bank was a tender for the 'Sea Lion'. Mistake number four was not recognizing that to keep this size of boat in such good nick that the saloon doors were oiled meant that there was someone aboard to do it – every day. Mistake number five was not recognizing that the echoing thud on the ship's stern was the dinghy coming alongside. Mistake number six was being there at all without telling Joe Steiner. But in this kind of set-up it's best to make a gallant attempt.

So looking surprised and cheerful I said, in the nearest approach to a public school voice that Birmingham would allow, 'I say old chap, I hope you don't mind me having a shufti over your boat. I'd heard it might be for sale.'

Kowalski was obviously not a man to be impressed by attempts, gallant or otherwise, or public school accents.

I was standing with my hands on my hips, which is the easiest way of looking relaxed without being relaxed. He came off the seat with his legs using the leverage of the bulkhead just like a swimmer turning in the baths, but he'd given the game away with a split-second flicker of the pale-blue eyes in the direction of my knees. When a guy does this there is a great temptation to do two neat steps backwards to leave him short, but if a man's got long arms it doesn't leave him short, and you've already assisted the momentum that puts you flat on your back. Anyway old habits die hard and I let him come on and shoved my knee up into his throat. It landed fair and square, and while he was fighting for breath I hacked my foot back up his face and there was a satisfactory crunching noise as it took out a few teeth. And as he was momentarily spreadeagled on the floor I remembered the Second Law of Aerodynamics as practiced by Special Operations Executive – to wit – if you have the chance, it is more effective to stand on a man's crotch than kick it. And that's what I did. Either this guy was out of practice or he'd had orders which didn't include killing. As I was making my orders up as I went along I reckoned it was better to be tidy, so I stuck my thumb deep into the pressure point under his ear and with a couple of jerks it was over.

There was almost no blood anywhere, but there were too many chances of his body being found accidentally for me to leave it lying around, and I was in no shape or mood to dig what was going to be quite a large grave. I went up on deck and had a look over at the dinghy. There were no signs that there had been anybody but Kowalski on guard. So I went down the jetty, across the island and dog-paddled over to *Samantha*.

When I got Joe Steiner on the phone he sounded like a man who'd been woken from a good sleep by a troublesome fly. When I'd broken the glad tidings to him it was well on in the conversation before he asked if I was all right. He phoned back ten minutes later and told me what to do.

I brought *Samantha* round and tied her up alongside Berger's boat, and I noticed for the first time that it was called *Magyarnet*. Getting the fourteen-stone Pole across the few feet and into the cockpit of *Samantha* was wearing on the arms and the spirit.

As I chugged to the closed lock-gates at Hurley there was the local bobby with his bike leaning against the lock-keeper's control, and having shone his torch to check on the name of my boat, he shone it on me.

'Can I come aboard, sir?'

We stood for a few minutes in the galley and he told me that arrangements had been made for me to go through Temple Lock and down to Marlow Bridge, and roughly two hours later there was a Royal Command Performance at High Wycombe Crematorium and Kowalski had the late night show all to himself. I had never realized before how few ashes got left behind, and that it takes twenty minutes for them to cool down. The director of the crematorium, who so far had been impressed by all the authority that had been floating round his head in the last two hours, found himself back on familiar ground and he was disappointed in my reply when he asked, 'Are the relics to go in an individual casket or in the Garden of Remembrance?' – and so that his professional pride wasn't hurt I stuck them in the third dustbin along myself.

Authority was arranged for me to go back up to my own mooring at Temple and by then it was 4 a.m., and although I was ready for sleep I was also ready for a good cup of tea, and whilst I was drinking it I realized that I really was back in the business. It wasn't until I was snuggling down in my sleeping bag that I remembered the sheet of paper from the pad in the little Palladian folly on Temple Island. I had a look at it under the bulkhead light and there was a good impression, and it said:

Plan 1900
Cobol
Fortran

Obviously some code, which wasn't up my street, so I laid it carefully in the locker under my bunk and went to sleep.

CHAPTER SIXTEEN

The next morning I swabbed down the boat. I think this was solely some psychological gesture because there was nothing to clean away. I spent an hour down at Meakes's boatyard at Marlow, filled her up with petrol and bought a few odds and ends from the chandlery. By the time I got back up to the moorings at Temple it was almost midday, and as I tied up against mooring number five, the sun came out. I stretched out on one of the lockers in the wheelhouse and decided to relax and think for the rest of the day.

About half an hour later the cooing wood-pigeons suddenly stopped and a herd of white rhino crashed through the bushes and I was able to identify it as Joe Steiner and Bill Autenowski who clambered grinning into the wheelhouse beside me and sat themselves down.

Joe was still grinning when he said, 'And how's the hero of the battle of Temple Island?'

'Fine, fine.'

'A bit drastic, wasn't it?'

'Well, what would you have done with him?'

Joe laughed. 'About the same, I think, if I'd had half the chance. More likely he would have done it to me. Anyway don't worry, Security Signals have been over the equipment and are delighted. There's no doubt that the transmitter is the one that's been used for most of the clandestine broadcasting that we have been monitoring over the last few months. I gather they fiddled around with it a bit which will help them keep tabs on it from now on. One of the interesting things they found out was that there is provision on the transmitter for a bloody great magnetic tape, and it seems that most of the traffic's been coming off these tapes.'

'Have they solved what the traffic's all about yet?'

'Not really, but what they do know is that it's in English. It seems to be in clear. The letter frequency is normal, there's no punctuation, and none of it makes sense. The brightest idea they've come up with so far is that it's some kind of routing instructions. I've told them that if they haven't broken it down in the next seven days, they are to have a meeting and go over it with the Joint Security Scientific Committee. Maybe a few fresh brains kicking it around could do the trick. Now is there any help that we can give you?'

'Yes, I want a talk with a bright computer guy. Somebody who'll know all about these peripherals that Berger sells, and I'd like the local police to be warned that I'll be going into Berger's office in the City and the warehouse he's got down by Putney Bridge.' Joe's face was screwed up in anguish. 'For heaven's sake, Ted, why the hell do you need to do it yourself. Have you got a touch of the 007s? We've got a dozen chaps who can go there and bring out anything you want. Why make a drama out of it? Use the resources we've got. Of course,' he added magnanimously, 'if you want to play cowboys and Indians, don't let me stop you.'

'O.K. Joe, it's a deal. I'd like copies of all invoices for the last year and the same for his bank statements. What about the computer expert?'

Joe scratched his head and looked across at Bill: 'Who do you think, Bill?'

'Well, I can have a word with IBM.'

Joe shook his head. 'No, I think we'll leave all the manufacturers alone. They're all pitching like mad at the moment for sales behind the Iron Curtain and we don't want to rock their boats. I'll have a root round, Ted, and get in touch with you this evening. Meantime, let's go and have some lunch.'

I took them down to La Chandelle in Marlow where Joe disgraced us all by asking for bacon and eggs. The chef actually appeared from his kitchen and the head waiter pointed at Joe and, with a stream of quite audible Marseilles abuse, the chef flounced back to his kingdom. They both left about two-thirty. About five o'clock there was a telephone call from Joe: 'About that expert, he's a guy named Claude Biggs. He's a software specialist, whatever

86

that is, and he works for an outfit called Computer Security Limited which, I might add, is nothing to do with us. He's completely secure and you can tell him what you need to tell him. He's yours day and night for as long as you want him but he's costing us eight quid an hour so don't bring us to financial ruin and, by the way, next time you're in that bloody restaurant give the chef my compliments. He doesn't fry a bad egg. Keep in touch,' and with no more ado the phone went dead.

I phoned Claude Biggs and asked him to come out and have dinner with me that evening, prepared to stay overnight on the boat. I sneaked down into Marlow and bought a children's book called *How Computers Work* (*Suitable for 8 to 12-year-olds*). Some people say that you're definitely growing old when policemen begin to look like young boys and buses seem to be faster, but I think the definitive indication that you're growing old is when you can't understand beyond Chapter 3 of a book written for schoolkids. By the time Claude Biggs arrived, I'd given up and decided to learn it all from the horse's mouth.

We stowed away his kit in the for'ard cabin and sat down in the saloon with a drink and he went over all the jazz about computers being very simple instruments; they could only say 'yes' or 'no' but they could say 'yes' or 'no' at about ten thousand goes a second. We went through the bit about how they were able to store information and repeat it and use it in a milli-second or something called a nannosecond which apparently made a milli-second a long time. There was still something missing as far as I was concerned but I decided to skip it.

'What are these peripheral things that Berger sells?'

'Well, peripherals are all the bits and pieces that enhance a computer's use. Things like terminals; you can hook these on to a normal telephone and link into a computer a hundred miles away, or a thousand miles away if you want. You've got disc drives which speed up the whole operation. You've got VDUs – Visible Display Units, they show on a screen what you're doing or the information that you've asked the computer for. Then you've got fast print-out machines that speed up your output – a bit like the telex that you see on your television screen that gives you the football results on Saturday evening but it works a hell of a lot faster. There's a hundred and one bits and pieces you can bolt on to a computer to make the work faster or more accurate or to enhance your storage of basic information.'

I passed him across a list of all the computer peripherals that Berger sold. 'Can you have a look down this, Claude, and tell me if there's anything unusual?'

He studied the list in silence for about fifteen minutes then shoved the list back to me and shook his head. 'No, these seem pretty run-of-the-mill things to me. It might be worthwhile me checking out that they are all that they say they are. Some of them are quite high-grade technologically, and all of them are made in East Germany as far as I can remember. They're pretty good at this sort of thing, far in advance of any of the other Iron Curtain countries.'

'Could you tell by looking at them in a warehouse whether they are what they say they are?'

'Pretty well on most of them but on the complex items, and there are only two or three of those, I'd need to play with them in the laboratory before I could check completely. On at least two of them the circuitry is so complex that I'd need instruments to sort it out.'

I passed the list back to him with a pencil. 'Can you mark the items you need to have in the laboratory?'

He marked three items. I tucked the paper back in my briefcase. I got us a meal and we chatted about life in general and retired to our respective quarters by ten.

I lay on my bunk and found I couldn't go to sleep because there was too much information churning round in my mind. Then I suddenly realized what the bit was that I didn't understand. I was opening my cabin door as Claude was opening the saloon door and we both arrived in the wheelhouse together. I noticed, inconsequentially, that we both patronized Marks and Sparks for their natty line in men's blue-edged briefs at thirty-five new pence a throw and we both said together, 'I've just thought of—' then we laughed and I said, 'Let's go down into the saloon, it's warmer,' and as we sat round the table again I waved to Claude and said, 'You go first.'

'Well, I've just realized there's one item on that list which I wasn't able to identify at all. It's just got a model number – R11 – and there's no description of what it does and I can't say for the life of me what the hell an R11 is. I've never come across it before.'

'O.K., Claude, we'll get you an R11. I've got a feeling you could have something there. Now the bit I don't understand is the middle bit. I can understand what computers do, I can understand what comes out of the other end on all this print-out paper. It's the bit in the middle I can't understand. How does the computer know what to do?'

'Well that's simple. You write a program telling the computer what to do.'

'You mean, you just say get on with the payroll or something like that.'

Claude smiled. 'No, it's not quite as simple as that. If you're going to do a payroll, the program instructs the computer to take the first name in alphabetical order and then you keep saying do this and do that. It's not complicated but you've got thousands of detailed instructions to write out and obviously they've got to be written in the correct order and you've got to keep referring it to where the appropriate data is stored. For instance, if you're telling it how to calculate a man's piecework earnings, you've got to tell it first how many hours of piecework he's done, what work he did in that time and then you've got to tell it where to look in the data bank for the piecework rates and how to relate it to the previous information and what to do with the calculation when it's made it.

'If you imagine going in a public library. When you go through the doors your mind decides whether it wants fiction or non-fiction and let's say you want fiction. Your data bank tells you where fiction is from past experience and when you've arrived in that section, if you're a computer, you'd sort out the first book on the shelf in the "A" section and you'd have to make all sorts of minor decisions. Have you read the book before? If "Yes" you pass it over, if

89

"No" does the name of the author ring a bell, does the title interest you? If not, pass to the next one and you've got to decide whether the next one is the next to the right or the next one on the shelf below. Every now and again you'll pick up a book that you may feel is interesting and find that although you didn't recognize the title or the author, you've read it before, so your memory was faulty. This never happens to computers. In fact, when you and I go in a library we wander about all over the place completely inefficiently, taking things at random but always somewhere we're using tiny bits of programming in our mind. With computers the basic thinking is done for them when the program is written and they never depart from this. When old ladies get gas bills for £10,000 it's never the computer that's wrong, it's the programming or the input that's at fault. Does that cover what you wanted to know?'

'More or less. How do these programs or instructions, or whatever you call them, get done. You say get written, how do you write them?'

'Well, programs are written in a computer language. There are several of these; there's one for commerce, one for engineering applications, there's one that mixes both capabilities and you also get variations of programming languages for different computers. For instance, IBM uses mainly three standard languages but ICL has what they call a configuration that uses an ICL language specially for their machines, and if you wanted to use one of the IBM languages on an ICL machine, you'd have to have what's called an interface to make the two different things compatible. Have you understood this?'

'Vaguely – when you say languages, you mean that computer people can speak to one another in a language that other people couldn't understand.'

Claude laughed, 'No, you couldn't really say that it's a language in that sense. For instance, in this country and America the computer language is written in English and that word "written" is important because until it's written down in the specialized form, they're just normal English words and figures, so if you read out a piece of computer programming it would be in English, but even to another computer man it would be meaningless unless he went over it step by step.'

'Could you write down a typical piece of programming for me right now?'

Claude hesitated for a moment. 'Yes, I suppose so. Any particular computer language you want it written in?'

I laughed. 'What have you got?'

'Well, let's take the most common one, Cobol.'

Suddenly I wasn't asleep any more 'How do you spell that?' and Claude spelt it out 'C – O – B –'

I held my hand up, 'Hold on Claude.' I padded back in my underpants through the wheelhouse into my cabin, bent down and lifted out the page that I'd removed from the pad at the folly on Temple Island and went back to the saloon. When I sat down again and held it slantwise to the light, Claude obviously thought I'd gone round the bend. Then I said to him, 'What's Fortran?'

'That's another IBM language with mainly engineering and scientific applications,' and pushing my luck I said, 'Does Plan 1900 mean anything to you?'

'Yep, Plan is the ICL language I was telling you about and 1900 is the description of their computer series that uses that language.'

'Just one more question, Claude. If you were selling these peripherals would you need to know anything about computer programming or computer languages?'

'No, not really. You just need to know about the configurations of the machines and your bits and pieces are either compatible or they're not compatible. What language is used on them is of no interest at all. You might have a client who uses a very low level language like Basic Assembler.'

I leaned back very pleased with the night's work. 'Claude you've helped a lot. Let's get to bed.'

I was asleep ten minutes later.

CHAPTER SEVENTEEN

I was awake by six o'clock and pulled on a shirt, an anorak, a pair of old jeans and a pair of rubber boat-boots. It was going to be a hot day and the mist was so thick you couldn't see the other side of the river. I couldn't even see the weir, but I could hear the water rushing over. The birds must have been having a long lie-in or they were foxed by the mist and thought it wasn't yet dawn. The jetty was slippery with dew and I rinsed my face and hands under the cold water tap on the bank. I dried myself on part of a toilet roll which gave me an idea and I shushed my way through the thick grass and the ferns to the brick-built toilet which the boatyard had provided for the customers at their posh moorings.

The loo and reading go together but the only thing in my pockets was the Thames Conservancy Rule Book and it's hard to take a real interest in all the lock dimensions from Teddington to Oxford. But sitting on a loo can produce great clarity of thought rather like being in an aircraft. As with impending execution, it concentrates the mind, and it always gave me the feeling that I could re-organize Imperial Chemical Industries and Eastman Kodak and then arrange a merger in well under twenty-four hours. On this occasion it took almost ten minutes for something to gel in my mind, and when I got back to the boat I phoned straight away to Joe Steiner. I was given another number to contact him which I recognized as one of the CIA hideaways in London, and it was good to hear Bill Autenowski's cheerful voice answer on the other end.

'Hi, Ted. How are things down your end?'

'O.K., Bill, but I'd like to talk to Joe urgently.'

'Sure. Hang on a moment, he's right here.'

'Joe, this list of peripherals that Berger sells, how was it compiled?'

'I'm not certain but I'm pretty sure that it was extracted from invoices.'

'Thanks, Joe. Have the boys done the job at the office or the warehouse yet?'

'No. We want to do them both on the same night and it's not scheduled for two days yet.'

'Well that's fine then. Joe, I may want to call that off, but meanwhile, can you check through the invoices and list all the companies that have bought a piece of equipment called R11. Would you mark at least four of them that you think could keep their mouths shut and co-operate.'

'O.K., Ted, when do you want this dope by?'

'Could it be ready by mid-afternoon today?'

'Anything you want, my boy, anything you want. Do you want it sent down?'

'No. I'll go up to my place in Chelsea and, if it's O.K. with you, I'd like to go through this with Claude and kick it around a bit. I'm certain now that it's the computer bit we're after and I've got a feeling that this R11 is important.'

*　　*　　*

The King's messenger from the Foreign Office handed over the thick envelope at three-fifteen. It was a list of twenty-two companies and six government departments, and there were pencilled kisses against three of the companies' names. There were photostat copies of invoices to these companies over the past twelve months. I gave half the photostats to Claude and took the other half myself.

'Claude, I've got a hunch but I think there's going to be something that links these outfits. They've all had R11s but they're going to have something else in common as well but I don't know what it is. So, if you will look through your pile, I'll look through mine and see if we can spot anything.'

After about ten minutes' shuffling, Claude said urgently, 'I've got it, Ted, I've got it. I don't know about your pile but in my lot R11s are never charged for. Every other item is charged for but there's just NC against that, which means no charge.'

'That sounds about right, Claude. Now let's just do a bit

93

of checking,' and I pointed at the three marked companies on the list. 'These are three companies who will co-operate with us. The easiest way of finding out what an R11 is, is to ring them up and find out and then you can go along and have a look at it. Who'd be the guy at their end to contact?'

'Almost certainly the Data Processing Manager. He'd be in charge of their computer installation. He'd have placed the order and he'll know what it does.'

'O.K., pal, you try them out.'

He went over to the telephone and was talking for about a quarter of an hour and when he hung up he said, 'There's no joy there, Ted. They swear they haven't ordered an R11 or received an R11 and they don't know what the hell it is either. The chap was getting very interested so I called it a day. I'll try the other two.'

He tried the other two with the same result, and he looked very glum when he said, 'Well, that's a wash-out, Ted.'

'Why?'

'Well we're obviously off on a false trail.'

'Not in a million years, Claude. Nothing could interest me more than a piece of equipment that appears on seventy-eight invoices, that nobody's ever heard of, nobody's ordered and nobody's received. That sounds like a very hot trail to me.'

He cheered up visibly. 'You're right, of course, but I'd never have thought of it that way.'

'Fair enough, I couldn't work a computer, you can,' and just as I said that the bells rang. 'Claude, your outfit's called Computer Security, what's it mean, what do you do?'

'I don't want to waste your time, Ted. Shall I send you round one of our brochures?'

'You're not wasting my time. I'd like to hear it right now.'

'There are two kinds of security that we cover, what we call physical security. A computer installation is probably the most expensive bit of machinery in most companies, and a fire, a flood or dust in the area, could bring the whole thing to a grinding halt. A bit of cigarette ash on a magnetic tape could screw up a whole payroll and that can mean a strike at Fords at Dagenham, but although this is important, that's pretty well a nuts and bolts area for us. We know it inside out and know how to deal with it. The other side is what's called software security, and that covers checking that a programmer hasn't written the company's payroll program so that he gets an extra ten quid a week, to very complex frauds which finance and insurance companies are wide open to. Then you've got sabotage, like a disgruntled employee who can wipe out every bit of data that the company has built up over three years in five minutes flat, by moving a small magnet over the magnetic tapes that hold their data bank. Then you've got the information itself. Any sales director would give his eye-teeth to have a look at his rival's sales accounts, up-dated so that they're only twelve hours old. You can even build up a hell of a lot of information from going over their payroll. It's a bit like the kind of things you chaps do.'

And when he said that I knew that the bells had been playing my tune. I knew I was almost there. I didn't know where 'there' was but I knew I was well on the way and I was so pleased I could hardly speak.

'Thanks, Claude, I'm going to take a short cut because I've got a feeling we need to be in a hurry. We are looking for a common factor in all these invoices and you were bright enough to notice that R11s were never charged for. We needed to know that but there's something else they've got in common. I don't know what it is but we'll swop invoices and go through them again. It doesn't matter how crazy it is. Anything that they've all got in common.'

Nearly an hour later, when we had swopped photocopies four times, we still hadn't got a clue and I was feeling very edgy, but this time Claude played the expert.

'Ted, we're wasting our time. If you'll agree, I'll take these invoices back to our offices. I'll get my best girl to punch cards for every bit of information there is. I'll cover the companies, what they do, what they use their computers for, where they are and all the stuff on every invoice. That will take about two hours. If they've got anything in common at all, the computer will throw it up in two minutes flat.'

I handed him my pile of copies. 'O.K., Claude, it's a deal. I'll sit here and wait. Don't phone me, come and tell me yourself even if there's no result.'

It was nine o'clock in the evening before he knocked on the door again and he was obviously bringing a success story. He could hardly wait to come out of the hallway. He handed back the photostat copies and a wadge of cards with holes in them, held together with two elastic bands.

'It's no wonder we missed it, Ted. The one thing they've all got in common is that they've all had terminals from Berger. They weren't always the same type or the same make and that's why we didn't spot it in just reading through the invoices. Too much for the old mind to catch hold of.'

'O.K., Claude, now tell me again what terminals do. These are the things you can plug into the phone to link yourself to the computer, aren't they?'

'Ten out of ten. That's exactly what they do. If you don't have your own computer, you can buy computer time from anybody. Mainly in off-peak times, of course, which means after midnight.'

I was sure that I knew what it was all about now, but I wanted to fill in the small gaps that were left.

'Do you know a lot about terminals, Claude?'

'Yes.'

'The construction and the technical bits, I mean.'

'Sure, I know them inside out.'

'O.K. Well, go to any one of the three companies you spoke to on the telephone and whip out their terminal and go over it with a fine tooth-comb. I'll fix it with Joe Steiner that they co-operate. I'll arrange an authority to supply them with any other terminal they want free of charge, and if they've got any moans and groans that you feel are genuine, do whatever deal you feel is necessary to keep them happy, and contact me as soon as you've got anything to say.'

'Can you give me a clue what I'm looking for.'

'Yes, I can give you three clues about what you are looking for but I'm not going to do it. We might lose out that way. I just want to know anything that you find different, or unnecessary, or that you can't explain.'

He told me which company he had in mind, and after he'd gone I contacted Joe to lean on Lord somebody-or-other, the chairman of a merchant bank.

CHAPTER EIGHTEEN

I'd arranged with Claude that I would not leave the flat until he contacted me, however long he might take, so by eight o'clock I opened a large tin of baked beans and ate them out of the saucepan. Conscious of my crude efforts, I decided on a very exotic dessert and, to two tins of strawberries I added a generous ration of Kelloggs' Cornflakes, and some latent culinary ambition drove me on even further to add half a tin of Nestlé's sweetened condensed milk. It looked rather like the magic potions that they give to racehorses when getting them fit for the Derby but it tasted like the smell of roses.

There was a TV documentary on, exposing the terrible behaviour of the CIA which took the team of interviewers to what must have been practically every sunny beach in South America. They never did catch up with a CIA man, but they interviewed many friends of friends who had first-hand knowledge of complex CIA operations in Alaska. It was a documentary by the BBC, mounted at enormous cost and, if you weren't an absolute moron, it faced you with the problem of working out whether this was British hypocrisy at its worst, or had the BBC really been taken over by Children's Hour.

The late night news on ITV brought the great tidings that unemployment was at its highest level yet, but a Government spokesman said there was no cause for alarm, as it was purely seasonal. The Department of Health had found in a recent survey that four out of five hospital beds in the United Kingdom were occupied by people with mental disorders, and the Tate Gallery had just asked the Arts Council for a grant of £75,000 to facilitate the purchase of the original Campbell's Soup tin painted by Andy Warhol.

The long-range weather forecast said that August would be a sunny month but showers were possible.

There was a frenzied outburst by an announcer about the

late night film, and it seemed that owing to popular demand we were to be treated to either the fifteenth or sixteenth screening of *Casablanca*.

I left the picture on but turned down the sound and set the alarm for 23·13 which, from past experience, I'd calculated to be exactly two minutes before Sam the pianist sat down at the piano and started playing 'As Time Goes By' which would cause Humphrey Bogart to come rushing in, and then Bogey would do a double or treble take at the limpid blonde standing unnoticed almost three feet away and, after a gulp, she'd utter those immortal words, 'Hello, Rick'. It seemed I hadn't allowed for the commercials, so I got an extra six minutes of dialogue.

Casablanca always gave me a great feeling of security, rather like my grandfather telling me that he could remember when Colmore Row was just a lane. Because I felt I was the last of the few who could remember when *Casablanca* was a brand new film. It was a bit like being a survivor from the Battle of Britain, and I could well imagine some Hollywood tycoon looking at the box office receipts and, thinking that he was saying it for the first time, announcing 'Never have so many owed so much to so few.'

It was about two o'clock in the morning when I realized there had been nothing on the screen for an hour except a small wobbly dot. I gave up hope of hearing from Claude and went to bed, and it was nearly midday when the telephone rang and turned the beautiful girl I was holding into a pillow. It was Claude.

'Ted, I need some help.'

'What sort of help?'

'I need a really top-level radio guy.'

'O.K., Claude. Don't say any more on the phone, I'll fix it. He'll be round to you fast.'

I spoke to the Duty Officer at Signals Security who wanted me to be more specific about the kind of expert I wanted. He finally conceded my ignorance but not before I gave him the old one-two and told him I'd let Joe Steiner know he was co-operating, and that seemed to do the trick.

Twenty minutes later I had a word with Joe and asked him to send round a typical sample of the monitored radio traffic. It was delivered about an hour later. It was in English but it certainly didn't make sense, though I was pretty sure it would make sense to Claude Biggs.

By ten o'clock the next evening I could wait no longer and I looked up the address of Computer Security Limited which was in a little mews at the back of Kensington High Street. I took a taxi to the Angus Steak Bar, then crossed the road and walked down the mews. There was no company plate at number seventeen, but when I pressed the bell, it was Claude who came to the door. He grunted, 'I wondered how long it would be before you came round.'

'Have you got anything?'

He didn't answer so I followed him through to the back of the building and he unlocked a door and ushered me in. There was a ginger-haired civilian working out an equation full of Greek letters on a blackboard, and alongside the equation there was an elaborate wiring diagram in several different colours. On a formica workbench there was what looked like the remnants of a large typewriter.

Claude's face was drawn and haggard, and when I asked him if he'd found anything I was quite certain that the answer was going to be 'No', but he looked up and said 'Yes, I've got what you're after, but I haven't been to sleep since I left you and I'm too bloody tired to go into the technicalities, but I can give you the gist of it if that's enough.'

I sat on a vacant chair and waited. Claude sighed as if the task of bringing it all down to my level was too much for him and he didn't look very hopeful when he said to me, 'Do you know what remote access is?' and he looked at me with surprise and renewed faith when I said, 'Sure, that's what makes my telephone ring when it's not plugged in.' 'You're dead right, Ted, you're dead right. There's a very advanced, beautifully sophisticated radio remote-access device in this terminal. You'd never find it if you weren't looking very hard, and what it does is....' I interrupted him, 'And what it does is to let anybody who knows how to activate it, take off everything the computer does twenty-

100

four hours a day, every day, and put it on magnetic tape.'

Claude's face flushed with anger. 'Look, mate, if you bloody well knew, I'll have ...'

I shook my head. 'I didn't know anything, Claude. I just guessed and put two and two together and made a hundred. You've turned the guess into know. I'm sure you'll get an MBE, or something equally pretty, next time the Queen has a birthday, probably under the heading of "For Services to British Industry".'

Claude looked quite impressed so I cashed in and said, 'I want another fifteen minutes of your time,' and I turned to the ginger-haired civilian who was still scribbling away. 'I'm sorry, I don't know your name. Thanks for your help but you can leave us now, and I just want to remind you that the Official Secrets Act applies as much inside the Service as out. So you don't discuss anything you've done tonight with anybody. If anybody wants to know, refer them to me.'

Claude let him out, and when he came back I handed him the monitored radio material. 'Can you tell me what that is?'

He looked at it through sleepy eyes, shook his head to wake himself up and looked again, but after about five minutes he shook his head and said, 'No. It doesn't mean anything to me. It's like a set of instructions split up by initials.'

I stayed silent for a few moments but he didn't have any more to say so I held my breath, crossed my fingers and prayed, and then said, 'Could it be a computer program?'

He concentrated on the paper for only seconds and then his head jerked up. 'For Chrissake, Ted, you're right and I've just realized what these initials are. Let me get some graph paper and I'll sort it out.'

Ten minutes later he threw his pencil on the table. 'Yes, it's a program written in Fortran and it's a program written for a production control system. I guess that it's for something in heavy engineering.'

'Could it be for a steel works or something like that?'

'Yes, could well be.'

101

'Thanks, Claude. Could you let me have a brief written report on the remote-access gadget and as little report as you need to do to explain how to disentangle this programming stuff.'

'Can I have some sleep before I do this?'

'Sure. How about you come down to the boat at about two o'clock today, and have the next day off at our expense and we'll have a quiet day on the river.'

I walked all the way back to King's Road, my mind in a whirl. A satisfactory whirl because I knew exactly what Berger was up to and we could clear the whole thing up in forty-eight hours flat and the powers that be could decide whether to knock off Berger or keep him in cold storage.

Back at the flat I stuffed clean underwear, some shirts and a spare pair of jeans into my hold-all, called for a hire car and told the driver to head for Marlow. I was asleep before we got on to the M4, and when I awoke we were in the centre of the town and it was six o'clock in the morning.

I paid off the driver and decided to walk up to Temple. Halfway across Marlow Bridge the sun broke through the mist. The tables with their gay umbrellas were still spread-eagled on the lawns of the Compleat Angler. On my side of the bridge was a line of boats for sale at Meakes's and they looked as though they were sitting on a sheet of glass. The water was absolutely flat except for the circles from early-feeding carp and perch. A pair of faithful swans and their two brown cygnets posed for next year's calendar. My watch said it was the 31st July and it looked as though the Met Office boys were going to be right.

It was nearly an hour before I got to the boat. I put my sleeping bag on the roof of the aft cabin and was asleep in two minutes.

What seemed a long time later I was suddenly wide-awake and I had a strong feeling that I was being watched. I carefully eased down the zip on my sleeping bag and squinted down at my watch. It was ten past ten. There was no doubt that in the strong sun on the white cabin deck I was very indecently exposed. I decided to go through the play-acting routine of slowly waking up. When I was sitting up and stretching my arms with my back to the bank, I knew I was being watched. A small hole in the middle of my back told me so. And I had a strong feeling that the hole in my back could be for real if I didn't do something about it. With some protection from the sleeping bag, I rolled from the cabin roof into the wheelhouse. Nothing was broken so I eased my way out of the bag and crouched against the port bulkhead. Part of the roof canopy was still hanging down and I pulled it slightly aside and looked out. There was no sign of anybody but you could have hidden a battalion amongst those trees and bushes. If there was anybody there, I was never going to see them unless they wanted me to, and it looked as though I was going to be pinned down until Claude came along at two o'clock, which meant four hours to wait, if he were dead on time. Then from over the starboard quarter I heard a nicely tuned engine turning out of the mouth of the lock, then turn towards the line of boats at the moorings.

The watcher wasn't going to do anything with any kind of audience, so I stood up in the wheelhouse and saw a Thames Conservancy Police launch coming alongside. The two river policeman looked friendly but suspicious, and it turned out that somebody had reported a stranger walking towards the moorings and, as there had been a lot of petty thieving, they'd like to see my proof of identity. My driving licence and AA card seemed to satisfy them, so to spin out the time I invited them aboard for a cup of tea. We compared notes about the riverside pubs from Maidenhead to Oxford and they were just clambering back into their patrol boat when the older one said, 'By the way sir, I notice you've got a sea-toilet fitted and you're not allowed to use this on the river, so I expect you'll be wanting us to seal it off for you. You can always break the seal when you get down below Teddington Lock,' and suddenly the world seemed a nice safe place when a policeman's only worry was the illicit use of a sea-toilet.

If the watcher had gone, I hadn't heard him go, but I felt at ease again and there was only another hour to go before Claude came at two o'clock. I telephoned Claude's number but there was no reply so I guessed he was at least on his way. I sat on the canvas chair in the wheelhouse and started putting the pieces together.

Berger's little gadget meant that they had continuous access to dozens of companies' expertise automatically provided for them on magnetic tape, which was then transmitted directly to somewhere behind the Iron Curtain from the transmitter on Berger's boat. It also meant that they had access to government department information on practically any individual who could be of use to them. They wouldn't need to contrive some blackmail information because they'd even have access to New Scotland Yard's confidential data-bank. It was all too clear why their trade missions were no longer interested in doing deals, they were getting day-to-day know-how on anything that interested them from us with almost no chance of the operation being uncovered, and Berger could have gone on supplying his masters with anything they wanted to know for the cost of a hundred terminals. I was going to enjoy the confrontation with Berger.

I was listening to the six o'clock news on the radio before I gave Claude another call, when I realized that there was something wrong with the boat. I rushed up to the wheelhouse and could see her bow turning to starboard out into the river and as my eyes searched in the gloom for the bow rope, I heard a car engine start and saw car headlights come on and a long dark estate wagon was heading down the pathway from the moorings. I walked round the gunwhales to the foredeck and saw the bow rope dipping into the water. Someone had untied the knots that held the rope to a tree. It was a senseless thing to do and easy to put right, and the worst that could happen was that my bow would rake the transom of the boat on the next mooring.

I walked down the planking of my jetty and crossed to the tree. The knots had been undone but the rope was loosely looped round the tree and went back into the water. I gave it a tug to fetch it back up but it was caught on some obstruction. I broke off a small branch and put a half-hitch round the stump and walked back to the boat for my torch,

104

and a knife to free the rope. A few minutes later I eased my way down the last couple of feet of the bank and shone the torch down the rope. It ended in a clove-hitch round a man's ankle. The man was Claude. And I didn't need to turn him over to know that he was dead.

It took me fifteen minutes to get him on the bank and I knew enough about the mechanics of rigor mortis to know that he'd been dead for at least three hours. He hadn't died of drowning. He'd been shot twice at close range. The first shot through his left eye would have been enough, for what must have been at least a ·38 bullet had taken out a four-inch jagged circle as it went through the back of his skull. The other shot had been through his left ear and he must have been falling or kneeling because the exit was through his neck.

Dumping him in the river tied to my mooring line was solely for my benefit. I supposed it must have been as a warning.

There was nothing I could do for Claude except find out whether you could have a posthumous MBE, but there was a lot I could do for Berger and it looked like it was time to do it. I walked down the pathway out of the mooring, down the lane to the junction to the telephone box, told the operator where I was and asked her to get me a car. It came fifteen minutes later and I told the driver to take me to the flat in King's Road.

CHAPTER NINETEEN

Despite the gun in my fist Berger looked at ease and, as if it wasn't my flat and my chair he was sitting in, he had the brass neck to make me at ease as well. A sweep of his hand graciously waved me to my own settee. A guy has to really have confidence to do that – and Berger had confidence all right. I was desperate to know why. It wasn't a bluff, he didn't expect to get shot, he wasn't going to be shot – he had decided that, not me. Despite the same craggy face he looked a hell of a lot smarter than when we had last met. A medium-blue suit in a lightweight cloth that looked good enough and expensive enough to have Dormeuil on the selvedges. One leg was casually over the other and he looked at me with a fairly cold smile and said, 'It's a long way from Hildesheim jail,' and it sounded like the title of a blues number – maybe I was thinking of Allentown. I didn't answer and I kept the automatic pointing at him. He looked at it and nodded towards it casually, and looking at me undisturbed he said quietly, 'I suppose you won't take my advice and put that thing down.'

I shook my head slowly. He shrugged and pointed at his inside jacket pocket. 'There's no gun in here, just a post-card, and I'd like to show it to you.'

'I'm not interested in postcards, Berger.'

'You'll be interested in this one.'

'Look – you're going to keep your hands on the arms of that chair, you're not to move an inch without I empty this lot into you, and I'm going to use the phone.'

Berger didn't move or speak as I lifted the phone. The handpiece came up easily because there wasn't any wire.

Looking cold rather than triumphant, Berger said, 'Look, Bailey, stop playing games. This place has been de-bugged by experts and that's for your own good – when you've seen this postcard you won't want to talk to Joe Steiner, you'll want to talk to me – may I show you now and we can start talking sense.'

'My dear Berger, I've got all I need to know about your operation and we'll have it bust wide open in less than forty-eight hours. It makes no odds to me or the rest of us whether you go in Wormwood Scrubs or whether you finish up on your back on my carpet. Your part in it is over and done with and you just don't matter any more.'

Berger looked at me for a few moments and then said, with venom in his voice, 'I can assure you, Bailey, that if you kill me, when you see the postcard in my pocket you will regret it for the rest of your days; but I will say this, if I wasn't acting under orders I could have had you finished off this morning, and right now if it were left to me I'd show you the postcard and let you squirm for the rest of your days.'

There was such a look of cold malice on Berger's face as he said this that I knew he meant it and the postcard must really mean something. If the KGB felt a postcard could outgun a gun it must be quite a postcard. Minor diplomats photographed in compromising situations with members of the crew of the battleship *Potemkin*, or whatever the Soviet Navy had these days, were easy game. So were members of trade commissions, photographed with compliant young ladies from Intourist, but I didn't come in either of these categories. I don't even like the British Navy, let alone the Russian Navy, and the failed ballerinas seconded to Intourist as easy lays for Western salesmen were far too skinny to interest me. Anyway, I had never been offered either. It obviously wasn't going to be a postcard showing the fortifications of Valetta Harbour, nor Karl Marx's grave at Highgate, and as these thoughts went through my mind, Berger was watching my face and knew I was rising to the bait.

Berger's smile was entirely with his mouth, and as I was thinking I noticed that Moscow was using much improved porcelain these days, and just as I thought this Berger said quietly, 'I'm thinking of someone,' and as I almost replied 'Dead or alive?' I realized that they must even know about the game that Sammy and I had played, and as far as I could remember we had always played it outdoors. When the other guy's unarmed, nowhere near as fit as you are, and you've got a 9 mm automatic with twelve rounds and one up the spout pointing at him it must be almost impossible to have a sinking feeling, but all the same I'd got one.

Berger and I looked at one another for what seemed a very long time and I knew he knew he'd won, and I knew he knew I knew it. All the trumps had been played but he was still going to trump my ace, and I knew I wasn't going to like it, but I didn't realize how much I wasn't going to like it. I held out my left hand and said, 'Give me the post-card.' He reached in his inside pocket and pulled out a colour photograph and handed it over to me.

It was of a girl about eighteen years old – to be exact seventeen years, ten months and four days. She was blonde with long hair, with a pert turned-up nose, a beautiful smile and very blue eyes, and when I'd last seen her she was four years one week old. I turned over the postcard and in a rather awkward script it said 'Dear Dadda, I'm told that a Mr Berger is going to make arrangements so that you can come and see me. All my love, Samantha.'

Way back in North Africa I was once foolish enough to tread on a land-mine but fortunately, because it was Italian, although it was beautifully painted it did no great damage, but I felt right now that I had trodden on another land-mine – made in Germany, Mk. IV anti-tank variety.

Although Berger must have known that I was going to get a shock and that this was the whole point of the exercise, for a moment he spoke almost gently. 'We picked her up in Brasilia. She has been taken good care of, had a first-class education in Moscow, and she is working now as an assistant editor at the Film Centre in Cracow. We have made arrangements for you to meet her in Warsaw and you could see her in two days' time if you co-operated.'

Somebody, somewhere had once said words to the effect that 'If given the choice of betraying my country or betraying a friend, I hope I'd betray my country', and I suppose I knew straight away that that's what I was going to do.

'What's the deal, Berger?'

He looked business-like now – 'We need another four weeks here. We'll take you to Warsaw and you and your daughter will be given safe conduct to any country you like, and a small pension.'

'And for the small pension I work for the KGB?'

Berger looked pleased. 'My dear Bailey, you've got a clever, intricate mind, and flair – which is important in our line of business – but we wouldn't employ you for five minutes in the KGB – the trouble with you is you think too much – when the chips are on the table it's dedication that counts. You have to be convinced by some fancy thinking – we just get on with the job. I haven't read *Das Kapital* or Lenin or Kerensky or even Dostoevsky. I do what I'm told – and I do it – like now.'

'How did your people pick up Samantha?'

'I've no idea, but if it's important I'll find out for you. We've watched your career with interest ever since you left the Army – we took it for granted that if ever I was uncovered they'd use you one way or another. So we took precautions.'

'I gather that what you've got in mind is that I'm removed to Warsaw and that after that Samantha and I are free to go.'

Berger looked at the automatic but I didn't move it away, so with a shrug he said, 'You realize that we can't allow you to have any further contacts in this country. If you want to do this deal we'll take you to an airstrip tonight and you will be in Warsaw tomorrow. We shan't interrogate you because there is nothing we want to know. We can fix for you to live in the Argentine, Cuba or Egypt, and they have no extradition arrangements with this country. Your pension will be worth about £2,000 a year and we'll pay you £4,000 cash for the things you've left behind. Although somebody will probably keep tabs on you, if you don't stick your neck out you won't get hurt. We've got a working arrangement with SIS and CIA in all these countries and they'll leave you alone as well.'

I suddenly realized that my real life was over. No more

London, no more Thames, no more boat, no more King's Road and no more England. All the long-term traitors like Philby and Burgess and MacLean are supposed to have missed England, but at least they believed in communism and that would never be for me. So I'd be an exile with a daughter who'd have her own life to live and who probably wouldn't remember me from Adam. But the scrawl and the words on the back of the postcard brought back all the memories of a small four-year-old blonde who waved me good-bye one morning and neither of us knew that I wouldn't be telling her the story of the rabbit and the strawberry jam that night, or any other night ever again.

It wasn't sense what I was doing but there didn't seem to be any choice. Every now and again you not only have to pay your own debts but somebody else's as well and this was one of those times.

I looked across at Berger to watch his face carefully. 'Why the big deal Berger, or would it be more fun dropping me in the North Sea than the Thames?'.

He took the point and responded quickly, 'You know as well as I do that I could have had you killed at Marlow if that's what my orders were. If you don't agree to our proposition, killing me won't save you. It may take a month or it may take a year but we'll do it. And we've got your daughter anyway. Moscow ordered me to make this deal and they are not taking all this trouble just to dump you in the North Sea or in the Moskva River.'

I tried hard to remember an exile from England who'd made it. I was no Oscar Wilde, or even a Byron, and the only one I could think of was P. G. Wodehouse who had found a tolerant acceptance in the United States.

One thing I could be sure of and that was that at the airport at Warsaw it wouldn't have up on a plaque, 'Send me your tired, your poor, the teeming masses from your shore,' and they wouldn't mean it either.

What they'd done to me in Magdeburg was nothing to what they could do on their own home ground and there must be a lot they'd like to know. But they'd done these kind of deals before and they generally stuck with them. They'd got Sammy – they'd seen her as a trump card and now they were playing her, there must be something they wanted or they could have just knocked me off – maybe just giving Joe Steiner the horse-laugh was enough. There were too many balls in the shooting gallery and my mind wouldn't sort it out.

I'd grieved too long and too often about the small blonde to give up even this slim chance of seeing her again, these boys knew it and I knew it too.

I pressed the release catch on the Browning, pulled down the cartridge case, pulled back the breech and the one up the spout flew out on to the carpet. They were lead-nosed and notched at their tips and I hoped that Berger either hadn't noticed or wasn't too well up on the Geneva Convention.

I laid the main frame of the automatic at the side of the chair and stood up. 'O.K., Berger, let's get started.'

And we got started the way he meant it to go on, because he waved me back to the chair and I sat down. He pulled up the briefcase from the side of his chair and handed me over my own passport. He then took out a small transceiver and pulled out an aerial about three feet long; in seconds there were bleeps like the BBC time signal. He just said 'Da' and pushed the aerial back into the body of the receiver.

I was reaching for the bottle of Glenfiddich when the doorbell rang. Berger indicated that I should answer it. It was one of the Poles – Jaworski – and he was dressed in a chauffeur's uniform which I suppose, with one embassy and another, must be the uniform most commonly worn by KGB officers abroad.

There was a few moments' talk in Russian between them, then we were on our way down the stairs. Half-way down Jaworski pulled out a key and we were suddenly in the half-gloom on some iron stairs in the church next door. Someone was playing the organ and I think he was playing Thalben-Ball's 'Elegy' – it was something I knew anyway. We went down into a basement that I had never realized was there, past some rooms that smelt of washing clothes.

111

Then we trooped through a garden and were suddenly in the shopping precinct by Sainsbury's.

It was late-night shopping day and the crowds were heavy; in case I thought it was all between friends, the chauffeur gave my left kidney a jar with the gun in his pocket.

There was a Ford Capri with the boot open parked on the double yellow lines. The boot was full of groceries for the benefit of any passing cop. The performance of the engine of the Capri would have surprised the guys at Dagenham. The way we took off caused great interest in the King's Road and a pain in the back of my neck.

CHAPTER TWENTY

We left the M1 at the turn-off for Bedford. We skirted the town itself, and as we headed what seemed to be due north I had no idea where we were. After about twenty minutes' fast driving we seemed to have done a big loop and the Capri took a sharp left bend and screamed to a stop in the dark in front of a five-barred gate covered with barbed wire and chicken wire. Despite the fact that it was overgrown with convolvulus and ivy, even in the dim light of the car's sidelights I recognized where we were and could not believe it.

I looked at Berger and he was already looking at me and genuinely smiling – 'A nice touch, Bailey, eh?'

The last time I'd seen the gate it had been politely manned by RAF police and Miliary Police, all very smart but not very security conscious because it was just a memorial service to the pilots and the people they had dropped who hadn't come back. The only other time I had seen it was when I was being dropped myself, oddly enough by a Polish aircrew, because this was the airstrip at Tempsford, hated or loved by members of Special Operations Executive during the war, according to whether they were going or coming back.

Half a mile on to the airstrip and the old shack was still there, but there were no lights, but there was enough moon by now to see a small Cessna four-seater with both engines already turning over. No duty-free cigarettes, no boarding card and no excess baggage – no baggage at all. There was no fancy stuff. We were all soon buckled in and it felt like the war all over again except that down below there were lights. Lights in houses where wives were waiting for husbands and lights from cars driven by men whose only worry was whether there was lipstick on their shirt collars, or whether they could really afford another washing machine.

But the lights were soon gone and we were over the North Sea and the journey seemed so long that I felt at one time that we must be flying direct to Stettin or maybe even Warsaw, but when we landed we were at the Russian military airfield just outside East Berlin. Like armed forces all the world over nobody was very interested in the four tatty-looking civilians. A KGB liaison officer took us straight to a Zim, and although he looked at me with some interest his main concern was to get us on our way.

It was really like old times when we ended up at a nice wooden house in the woods. I was shown to a decent-sized room with no windows and the door was discreetly locked behind me. It must have been some sort of top-level international KGB transit camp, because the books on the bookshelves were in many languages and most of them would not have been acceptable even to the Tsar of All the Russias, let alone the present incumbent. The newspapers which were spread on a large table covered all Europe and they were today's issues. Even the *Wall Street Journal* and the *Washington Post* were only one day old. There was a copy of the *New Statesman* and Richard Crossman was tearing up the Labour Party and Alan Watkins was putting it together again. Somebody had side-lined in ink some particularly vitriolic statements.

By the time I'd got to the Letters to the Editor, Berger came in followed by a girl wheeling a tray of food. She was very blonde, very pretty and after saying, in perfect English, 'If there is anything else you'd like, sir, please let us know,' she gave an old-fashioned curtsey and left the room.

Berger was indulging in a long cigar, and from the beautiful smell it probably came back on one of the missile ships from Cuba. He indicated that the Rhine maiden was available to save me from a lonely night, and as an alternative offered to play me at chess. We played whilst I was eating, and despite his rather corny Queen's Gambit and a bit of fumbling in the middle game, he beat me quite easily. He seemed in no hurry to go so I asked him what the programme was for the next day and I tried not to flinch when his friendly hand patted my knee and he said, 'We'll be leaving for Warsaw about eleven and we've made arrangements for you to stay at the Grand Hotel and you will be seeing your daughter about four in the afternoon. We thought you might like two or three days with her in Warsaw and after that it's up to you. All the arrangements will be made for you by Intourist.'

I managed a wan smile – 'With just a little leaning on by the KGB, I suppose.'

He had obviously read his Winston Churchill and was generous in victory, and with an expansive wave of his cigar and the best grin he could muster, he said, 'We're always willing to help any department of the State.'

I'd taken my jacket off and was sitting on the edge of the bed, and as Berger's grin faded we looked at one another for what seemed a long time and for a ghastly moment I saw pity registered in his cold eyes. I wasn't used to being pitied, I didn't like being pitied and I hated being in a position where it was possible for a bastard like Berger to be able to pity me. My resentment probably showed in my face, and with a wave of his hand and the stub of his cigar, he walked briskly out of the room and the key turned on the other side.

All over the world intelligence services must thrive on and enjoy their attention to detail, because on the bedside table was a bottle of Glenfiddich and a Thermos flask, and when I opened the lid of the flask it was beautifully made fresh hot chocolate. As I only had the clothes I stood up in, I overcame my normal inertia about clothes and moved over to the wardrobe to hang the trousers and jacket up. Inside was a shelf with six Marks and Spencer's shirts still in their cellophane wrappings and my size. There were two lightweight suits, brand new, both with Daks labels in them, and they were my size too. As I unlaced my tie and lodged it on a hook I noticed the parachute motif on it and the complete incongruity of the whole situation came home to me. It must have been the first time that a Special Forces Club tie had hung in the wardrobe of a KGB transit house. Eton ties, yes; Harrow ties, maybe; but Special Forces Club ties – that I couldn't believe.

The whole world of spies and counter-spies which seems so powerful to the outsider all comes down in the end to men and women who love or hate other people, who are moved or left cold by Elgar or Tchaikovsky or Barber according to their characteristics or nationality, but at the end of the day, as Harold Wilson would put it, you were in a room somewhere, and then you were on your own. Not just in your body but in your mind. Small trivial things move your mind more than revolutions, earthquakes and assassinations, and the SOE tie seemed to me to epitomize the beautiful pathetic strivings of western civilization where ex-spies and ex-counter-spies had friendly little clubs so that you could try and pretend that you're normal and it all never happened.

I felt pretty sure that there wasn't a club in Moscow for ex-members of the KGB unless it was the cemetery at Pokrovsky Cathedral, and I hoped without hope that some defecting KGB man was sitting in a room somewhere in London or, more likely, Oxford, looking at the ribbon of his Order of Lenin and missing whatever it is that Russians miss.

In the car and on the plane things were happening to distract the mind, but as I pulled the covers of the bed up to my chin I had the feeling that I wasn't going to sleep much that night.

I was wrong, of course, because the ability to sleep no matter what the situation was part of my stock in trade, but before my eyes closed my mind had gone over what it would be like when I met young Sammy again the following day and where would she want to make our home. I went over a dozen opening sentences which ranged from the bright and breezy to the pathetic and it was at this point that I must have fallen asleep.

CHAPTER TWENTY-ONE

The prisoner was offered a hearty English breakfast next morning but I didn't use it apart from the strong black coffee. I dressed in my old suit, and the Rhine maiden packed the rest of the clothes in a small leather case. About an hour later we were boarding a scheduled flight of LOT, the Polish National Airline. About two hours after that we were circling Okiencie Airport, outside Warsaw. There was a large black Mercedes waiting for us there and we were joined by two obvious KGB men in plain clothes who were clearly very senior to Berger, and as we moved from the airport the signpost said 'Warszawa'.

Berger was getting a flood of congratulations. There was a lot of colloquial Russian, much slapping of thighs and hearty laughter rather reminiscent of England having beaten Ireland at Twickenham. Everybody was very pleased with themselves, except me.

Even the road into Warsaw was communist; long, straight, boring and predictable. The flat fields stretching out on either side soon gave way to new blocks of flats, and after about twenty minutes we swept into Ulica Krucza to the front entrance of the Grand Hotel. There were no formalities and I wasn't booked in and it was a lot more modern that I had expected. We went up to the fourth floor and nobody showed us the way as we tramped down a long, thickly carpeted corridor I still had enough bloody-mindedness to make some effort to keep out of step with the rest of the entourage. A very large door took us into the sitting-room of an attractive suite and we were really in Poland because the décor came straight from the film set of *Maria Walewska*.

There wasn't a baritone or a tenor in sight, but sitting on a beautifully embroidered chair was Audrey Hepburn, or if it wasn't her, you could have fooled me, and it came as something of a shock when Berger introduced me to her and I found her name was Grazyna Kujawska and he explained that Miss Kujawska was in the adjoining suite and was a member of Intourist. It seemed she could speak excellent English, already knew Sammy, knew all about the set-up and would be making the arrangements for our onward travel. What he didn't mention, but I would have bet the last pound of my KGB pension on, was that she never shot less than 98s at 25-metres and that any man outside the KGB who made an unacceptable pass would fly through the air with the greatest of ease and to his dying day would believe that that fragile hand and only 275 hours of training were responsible for it.

Everybody made themselves at home and I was a bad host. I had seen this film many times before and I knew just how Cary Grant or Jimmy Stewart would have played it, but I hadn't got a hat to stick on the back of my head, I wasn't wearing an old raincoat and I didn't feel up to rocking on my heels.

Miss Kujawska came to my rescue and patted the seat of the armchair next to hers and I obliged. Cigars were lit, cigarettes were passed round and then there was a silence and Berger said, nodding at the taller of the KGB men 'Let me introduce you to Colonel Petrov – he'a a full colonel, by the way.'

I suppose English majors should feel honoured when interviewed by Russian full colonels. Anxious to display his wares, Berger explained that Colonel Petrov had been to Magdalen College, Oxford, and just to put me down, he pronounced it correctly. Colonel Petrov, from his smile, was a traditionalist – there were three or four very fine stainless steel teeth displayed in his charming smile when he said, 'And how's Joe Steiner these days?'

The big muscular frame was quite relaxed and his smile quite unperturbed when I sat silent; it seemed almost as if he were echoing my thoughts when he said: 'Ah, Berger, our friend's a traditionalist – he remembers all that jazz about name, rank and number,' and, jabbing his finger at me, he said: 'Don't worry, we'll stick to the deal and we won't ask any questions. I gather from our friend Berger that you

118

nearly did a very good job – in fact,' he said generously, 'I gather if it hadn't been for your daughter you would have completed a very good job,' and he leaned back, half closed his eyes and said, 'Wasn't it Oscar Wilde who said "He rides the fastest who rides alone?"'

I touched his sword gently with mine and said, 'Actually, the quote is "He travels the fastest who travels alone."'

'Ah, yes,' he said, 'you are quite right.'

I didn't know why they were pulling the Magdalen College bit but I knew despite the impeccable English and the BBC accent that there weren't that many alumni of Magdalen who would attach Oscar Wilde's name to a line of Rudyard Kipling; neither author would have been amused.

Petrov stopped sipping his vodka and rested his glass on his knee. 'When you and your daughter have decided where you want to live one of my people will visit you – just for a talk.'

'You'd be wasting his time, Colonel. I'm not a defector.'

The big fingers scrabbled confidently in his short hair while he looked across at me not merely unabashed but positively bored.

'Bailey – you're not a fool. Berger could have had you killed days ago if that was what I had wanted. Instead we've arranged something contructive for you. I've already told you that we don't expect or even want you to work for us. However...' and his fingers gently squeezed the soft leather of his cavalry-style boots '... however, there is something that I shall ask you to do,' and although I had made no move to speak he held up a silencing paw, '– nothing to do with espionage but to my country's advantage and to your motherland too – you can decide if you'll co-operate when the times comes.' Hearing England described as my motherland sounded odd and I had a fleeting vision of the Household Cavalry, flags and Henry the Eighth. I looked across at Petrov but he wasn't even looking in my direction. He glanced at his wrist-watch and stood up.

Nobody gave a signal but everybody else got up including Miss Kujawska, and as I sat there, Berger patted me on the shoulder and said, 'Maybe I'll see you again before I

119

leave, or before you leave. If you want to get in touch with me Miss Kujawska can fix it. We shall be keeping an eye on you but we shan't be making a nuisance of ourselves, but it would help a lot if you would stick to Miss Kujawska's instructions. You may be sure she will have your interests at heart,' and Miss Kujawska herself looked as if she actually believed it.

Everybody trooped out of the room and I was left with the lady from Intourist who, as she closed the big door behind them, turned round and, leaning back against it, said 'Men don't think about these things but let me say it – welcome to Poland.'

She moved and sat in one of the chairs facing me and, pouring out coffee from a silver pot, she looked up at me and said. 'I had in mind that I'd arrange for you to see Sammy this afternoon as I thought you might like a rest after your journey.'

I looked over at her. The resentment that I'd felt for years faded away. I'd always felt that it was a dirty trick that Audrey Hepburn had got the part of Eliza Doolittle in the film version of *My Fair Lady* instead of Julie Andrews, and I'd never seen the film on that account, but as I looked at Miss Kujawska, I felt that they were right. The little fringe, the pert nose, the wide generous mouth and the big soft eyes that hit my own like a beam from a laser were so gentle and so feminine that for a moment I believed that she had my interests at heart, and if I'd been a casting director for MGM she could have played Tarzan if she'd wanted it. I kept my eyes away from her face.

'How is Sammy?'

The big green eyes flecked with hazel looked into mine and, ignoring my question, she said, 'According to our records you spent a lot of money and a lot of time looking for Sammy when she was taken away. You must have loved her a lot.'

'Yes, I did love her a lot. I still do. Part of it was selfish; I missed her a hell of a lot. Where've you fixed for us to meet?' I asked.

'I thought it would be best if you met here.'

'What made you think that?'

'Well, the last time you saw her she was a very little girl, only just four, now she's a young woman with a career and a place of her own and, although I know you know all this, I felt it still might be a bit of a shock to you when you came face to face with it.'

I looked across at Miss Kujawska. 'You seem to have given this a lot of thought.'

She held my glance for a moment and then looked down at her hands and for the first of many times I noticed how calm and gentle was her face, and I sensed that she was aware that I was looking at her.

'I have been studying your case history for a month in preparation for this meeting and it's part of my responsibility to make it as easy and as simple for you as I can, and we'd both be very stupid if we didn't recognize that this is not going to be easy for either of you after all these years. One of our department psychiatrists produced an evaluation of you and it said that both in your work and your emotional life there was a strong feminine streak in your make-up which served you well in your work but badly in your personal life, and I don't want anything to spoil that from now on.'

'Makes me sound like a cross between Bing Crosby and Shirley Temple.'

'I don't think your war record substantiates that,' she said.

I noticed a small opal ring on the third finger of her left hand. 'Are you a Scorpio?'

She frowned. 'What's a Scorpio?'

'It's a sign of the Zodiac of people born in the thirty days from the 24th October.'

She laughed and clapped her hands: 'We don't have such foolish things in modern Poland but I can remember my grandma talking about these sort of things when I was a little girl. My birthday is 18th April, whatever that means in your signs of the Zodiac, but my grandma gave me this ring and her birthday was the same as yours.'

'Which is?'

'24th October.'

'You've got a good memory. Where does Sammy live?'

'Number 17 Ulica Wczasowa. She's got two rooms in a block of flats.'

'Must be pretty important to have two rooms.'

'No, it's not extraordinary in Poland, even in Warsaw.'

'You must have a better Housing Ministry than they have in Moscow then.'

She involuntarily glanced at the bowl of flowers on the table between us and I took the hint and wondered how she'd reply, and for some reason I was slightly chilled when she said, 'Maybe that represents a sacrifice by the Soviet Union for the benefit of Poland.'

I didn't press the point, and after a few moments' silence she said, 'There's time for you to have at least two hours' sleep before Sammy arrives so I'll leave you, but if you need any help or want to speak to me there's a direct line from your room to mine on the green telephone by the side of your bed. The red telephone is for any outside calls you may want to make.'

I laughed, 'I don't speak any Polish and I don't know anybody in Warsaw.'

She said very quietly, 'There are at least four people in Warsaw you know whom you may like to speak to.'

Still smiling, I counted on my fingers, 'Berger – I don't want to speak to him. Sammy – not till I've met her anyway. You – O.K. Who is the fourth?'

And it was like a bucket of cold water when she said, 'Bob Fraser.'

I realized my voice was very flat when I said, 'Is he still alive?'

'Yes, he's still alive but he's in prison. He does useful work editing an English language newspaper.'

And suddenly we were on opposite sides and I said grimly, 'Why didn't anybody let his wife and family know that he's still alive and put them out of their misery?'

There were two scarlet spots on her cheeks and she said: 'I'm afraid that's no business of mine,' and a few moments later the door closed behind her – loudly.

I made a mental note to go and see Patsy Fraser as soon as I got back to England – then I realized that I was never going back. As I took off my jacket, loosening the knot in my tie, I lay back on the bed and worked out that I could send her a letter from wherever I ended up, and that masterpiece of logical thinking must have sent me to sleep.

CHAPTER TWENTY-TWO

I had written a dozen little story-boards in full colour with all the versions of how to go about making Sammy feel at ease with me when we first met. They all started off with me freshly shaven, clean shirt and suit, all purveying an impression of self-assurance and the sort of father that all girls dreams of. But it didn't turn out that way.

When I woke up I glanced at my watch – I'd been asleep for over four hours and as I went to move my right hand to push back my hair I realized it wouldn't move and as my reflexes made me turn quickly, a voice said, 'Don't worry, Dadda, it's only me.'

Sammy's two hands were holding my hand and as I looked at her all I could think of was what a tatty unkempt man I must look. My mind just wouldn't work and I could think of nothing to say. I didn't even say 'Hello' and then suddenly she was kissing my face and the long blonde hair brought back the flood of memories and I was crying and we were hugging one another.

Then I pushed her up and leaned up myself on one elbow and we just looked at one another and I said, 'I've missed you Sammy, I missed you.'

She opened her mouth to speak and I was sure she was going to say she'd missed me too and suddenly I was a man again. I put my fingers on the soft young mouth and said, 'Sammy, I know you can't have missed me. We don't have to pretend with one another; we know what happened and I'm just glad you're here with me now. I'm going to change and I'm going to order us a meal. Then we'll just talk.'

She nodded. I swung my feet off the bed and while I was shaving she leaned against the bathroom door and watched me. She was tall, as blonde as she was when she was a little girl, very beautiful and shaped like a young woman, not a little girl, and I found that surprising.

'How long had you been sitting on the bed?'

She looked at her watch. 'Oh, just over an hour.'

'Well, that wasn't how I'd planned it.'

'Dadda.'

'Yes.'

'I do remember things about you despite what you said.'

'Tell me what you remember.'

'I can remember you waking me up and taking me out to see the moon because you thought it was beautiful. I can remember a story you told me about a rabbit and strawberry jam. I can remember you taking me to see goldfish in a pond somewhere near where we lived and I can remember being with you on a boat and the sun always seemed to be shining – I can remember lots of things, just little things.'

I carried on shaving because I couldn't speak, and after a few moments I said, 'Did they tell you why I'm here and what it's all about?'

'I don't suppose they told me everything but I gather it's something to do with the KGB and that you've changed your mind – politically I mean – and that you are now helping the Soviet Union.'

I turned round and looked at her and was conscious that I was wagging my razor towards her. 'Sammy, if they said that, they're kidding. I haven't changed my mind politically because I don't give a damn about politics. It's people that matter, and whatever country you live in you're stuck with the system they've got. I wouldn't lift a finger to help the so-called communists. I'd better say right now that I'd bet my last dollar there are about ten microphones bugging this place, so you needn't give me the standard party line, just say nothing and let's leave it at that.'

I realized I was looking at her intensely and angrily and she suddenly looked a very little girl. I put my hand on her shoulder. 'Sorry, Sammy, I'm being the domineering father after only five minutes. I've no right to be and I don't mean to be. I've got a pretty open mind about politics but I suggest we forget the subject altogether. Let's talk about us and what we're going to do. Did they tell you the countries we could live in?'

'Yes.'

'I think I can guess which one you'll choose.'

She smiled. 'Tell me then,' and I smiled back as I wiped the lather from my face.

'Oh, I think you'll want Cuba with all those dark handsome men with Castro beards.'

She laughed, 'Dadda, you're like all men. You think that women think about nothing except men and even then in terms of flashing eyes and curly hair. We're not brought up like that over here, you know. We have to care about everybody, the whole people, and we care about the work we do and whether it's useful . . .'

I interrupted, 'For heaven's sake, Sammy, let's stop lecturing one another. Let's go and order a meal and, if they've got it, let's have a bottle of real champagne. Do you think they'll have champagne?'

She squeezed my arm and said, 'From what I gather, you're important enough for them to get champagne if you want it.'

They had got champagne, it was the first time that Sammy had ever tried it and she obviously wasn't that impressed, but the meal was excellent and she tucked into that with gusto. During the meal she told me about her work at the Film Centre, and it was obvious that she was competent and really interested in her job.

'What kind of films have you been concerned with so far?'

'Well, I've edited two documentaries myself; one about the steel industry and one about the rebuilding of Poland. I was assistant editor on a comedy that won a prize at Cannes and right now we're shooting an old-fashioned love story. I've been working with a film crew and the director to learn about that end of the job.'

'Do you know, Sammy, I can't even remember what day it is.'

She laughed and said, 'It's Sunday.'

'What would you be doing on a Sunday evening if I wasn't here?'

'Well, if you weren't here I shouldn't even be in Warsaw but if I were I'd probably be going for a walk in the park.'

126

'Is it a nice park?'

'Yes, I think so. It's rather old-fashioned and a bit romantic and I think you'd like it.'

'Why don't we go then?'

After about a twenty-minute walk we got to Lazienki Park. The giant palm trees had been brought out from the hot-houses and set out in their tubs on the grass. As we walked to the end of the lake there was a ruined palace and Sammy told me that it had been built for one of the last Polish kings and that it had been partly destroyed during the war by the Germans. A little way from the lake was a statue of Chopin seated under a weeping willow. There were benches round the statue and we sat there and watched the red squirrels and I held hands with Sammy, and despite what I'd said before, I couldn't help asking her something because I needed to know.

'Sammy, would you find it difficult if we lived in a non-communist country?'

She looked at a squirrel for a long time before she replied, then looking at me said, 'Can I ask you a question before I answer?'

'Sure.'

'Will you tell me what you really think of communism.'

I grinned back at her and said, 'I think you're going to be shocked.'

'We're never shocked about what foreigners think about communism,' and I noted the 'we' and I noted the 'foreigners'.

'Well, seeing that you asked me and that you're unshockable, let me say I've always felt that communism would work. The only snag is nobody's ever tried, nobody's ever had the courage to try it.'

She looked puzzled. 'But surely the Soviet Union . . .'

I cut across what she was saying, 'They didn't even try communism, they just turfed out a monarchy then clobbered any intellectuals who were around and the louts took over.'

'You talk like a typical capitalist.'

'I can assure you I don't, because I'm not a capitalist. I

127

haven't any capital, I don't employ anybody. Like you, I'm a worker. I live in what's described as a capitalist society and it's got a hell of a lot of faults but it's got one great virtue and that is that if my doorbell rings at two o'clock in the morning, it's going to be the people next door asking me to turn down the hi-fi, not the KGB.'

'Don't the CIA ever press doorbells at two in the morning?'

'Sure they do, but they'll have a warrant in their hands if they are going to arrest you that's been signed by a judge who's not a politician. You can have twenty-five attorneys to defend you if you want and every newspaper in the land will be watching out for some infringement of justice and they'll be shouting their heads off in your defence if they get half a chance.'

Sammy was silent and in the end I had to say, 'Why don't you say something?'

Sammy smiled. 'I think I'm going to say something that's going to shock *you*.'

'Say on then.'

'Well, I meet a lot of Americans, admittedly they're mainly from the film industry and they may not be typical, but I think they're very like the Russians. They love children, they bother about education, everything has to be on the grand scale, everything's got to be bigger or quicker or better than the next man's and the only thing that makes them different is their complete assurance that the other man's system is wrong.'

I laughed. 'I've been saying for many years that it won't be too long before the Russians and the Americans are allies because they've got so much in common that it's inevitable.'

Sammy looked at me quizzically, 'You really have got an open mind, haven't you, Dadda?'

'No, I'd be a liar if I said I had. I don't like the Soviet system and I never will. I think its an outrage and an exploitation of human beings and nobody's ever going to convince me that the end justifies the means. Adolf Hitler tried that and the people who've run the Soviet Union for the last fifty years have been just as much maniacs as he was. They've just been more successful.'

Sammy shivered slightly in the light breeze and I squeezed her hand.

'Is where you live very far from here?'

'No, about ten minutes' walk.'

'Well, how about you taking your old father back and giving him a cup of coffee.'

'That would be fine, let's go.'

Ulica Wczasowa was a block of flats that you can only describe as human battery cages, but you could see just the same in Birmingham, Manchester, Philadelphia and Minneapolis – give or take a lick of paint the new brutalist architecture seems to be universal.

Sammy's two rooms were bright and very feminine. I sat on the end of her bed while she made the coffee. There were some certificates pinned up on the wall but they were in Russian script and I couldn't make out what they were for. There were a dozen books on her shelf and, as far as I could see, all of them were textbooks. On the window-ledge was a vase with some chrysanthemums and a glove – a man's glove. Then Sammy turned round beaming, and as I looked at the tray, I saw why. There were two mugs of hot chocolate.

I grinned up at her. 'Those boys have their uses don't they?'

After we'd had drinks she explained to me how to walk back to the hotel and we arranged to meet for lunch at the Bristol the following day. I kissed her good-night at the outside door and then closed it behind me.

I'd only walked about a hundred yards down the street when I heard footsteps running after me and as I turned I saw that it was Sammy, and as she came up to me she held the lapels of my jacket and I could see that there were tears on her cheeks.

'Oh Dadda, I can't go to sleep without asking you something.'

I pulled a handkerchief out of my pocket and said, 'Whatever it is there's no need to cry,' and I dabbed the

129

tears away as I'd sometimes done when she was a little girl. 'Well now, what is it that you want to tell me or ask me?'

Her look was very intense. 'Would you consider staying in Poland?'

I bought a few moments time to think. 'Would they let us?'

She nodded, 'I think they would if you said you wanted to. You've been against them for a long while but all the same I think they respect you.'

I slid my arm in hers and walked her back to the entrance door to the flats. I put my hands on each side of her face and kissed her and said, 'I'll think about it and we'll talk about it tomorrow.'

CHAPTER TWENTY-THREE

When I got back to my room at the hotel there was a card on the bedside table which said 'Hope you had a good time with Sammy, Love Grazyna', and there was a bathrobe on the bed and some pyjamas.

I got undressed and was sitting in the bathrobe in one of the comfortable armchairs smoking when there was a light knock on the door and I shouted, 'Come in.'

It was Miss Kujawska. She was wearing a black woollen sweater and black trousers. 'I just came to see if you were all right.'

I returned the compliment of earlier in the day and patted the armchair beside me, and without playing coy she came round and sat down.

'By the way, there aren't ten microphones in your room. There's only one and I'm the only person who monitors it. I haven't been asked to report on any details of your conversations, just to use my discretion.'

I looked at her, smiling. 'And how much discretion have you got, Miss Kujawska.'

'Oh, a lot. I care about you and your daughter.'

'I can understand why you care about my daughter but why should you care about me?'

She frowned. 'Well, I'd read a lot about you before you came here and I felt I knew you well, almost as if we were old friends, and I wondered if you'd be like what I imagined.'

'And was I?'

'Yes, you're even nicer.'

For some reason I liked that bit. If I ended up nicer, I must have been nice to start off with.

'Can I ask you something about Sammy.'

'Of course.'

'Is she a party member?'

'No. She has Soviet citizenship but she isn't allowed to be

131

a party member and I don't think she's very interested any-way.'

'Who's the man?'

She looked baffled. 'What man?'

'There was a man's glove in Sammy's apartment.'

'Oh, I see. Did she not mention a man to you?'

'No, but I'd like to know who he is.'

'Do you think it's fair that we should talk about her pri-vate life. Don't you think that if she'd wanted you to know, she'd have told you?'

'Not necessarily. Maybe she'll tell me anyway. This is only our first time together and there's a lot I don't know yet, but she asked me tonight if it would be possible for us to stay in Poland and I guess this man is part of the reason or all of the reason, so I'd like to know all I can.'

'Would you consider staying in Poland?'

I shook my head. 'No, never.'

'But you'd understand if Sammy wanted to?'

'Of course, she's my daughter and I love her.'

Her small right hand came to rest on my arm, 'The man's name is Yuri, Yuri Gregorov. He's a writer. He's a Russian from Moscow.'

'What's he doing in Poland?'

'He's writing film scripts.'

'So I suppose he's one of those blond football-playing types but with a dacha just outside Moscow.'

Her fingers squeezed my arm and she smiled. 'No, I'm afraid you're wrong on all counts. His hair is grey like yours. I'm sure he was never good at sports. He's out of favour with the Ministry of Culture and working at our film institute is for him about the same as being sent to the Foreign Legion. He's not very much younger than you, he's about forty-five or forty-six. He taught literature, Russian literature, at the high school Sammy went to.'

'Do they live together.'

She nodded, 'I think so.'

'Does she love him?'

'Yes, she loves him very dearly and he loves her too.'

I lit another cigarette and offered her one but she refused.

A few minutes later she said good-night and left me on my own.

Like Paris and the French, the war had left Warsaw grey and soulless. Just a place, with no spirit. I hated it more as each day passed, and although we were only in August, the weather changed to match my mood and the wind blew the first leaves from the trees.

Over the next three days Sammy and I were together most of each day. I said nothing about Yuri, neither did Sammy, but each day I was more and more aware that the whole idea of us going off together was impossible. She had a life that obviously fulfilled her. She had a man she loved, and if I took this away it would be pointless and selfish. I wasn't even sure any longer that she'd come but I was sure that if she did it would only be from a sense of duty. The sick spite that took her away had done what was intended. The small girl who had been so defenceless had had to build her own defences and it seemed to have succeeded. If she came away with me they'd fall apart. When I'd finally lost track of her I'd had to face the fact that there was nothing I could do – for her or for me, and I had that same feeling now. Way back I needed her and she needed me. Right now others mattered to her. I was a piece of history, a reminder of past unhappiness, and as we talked cheerfully to each other we were both aware that there wasn't much sand left in the top of the egg-timer.

Every night when I got back to the hotel there was a note from Miss Kujawska and a knock on the door. I couldn't bring myself to tell her much of my feelings about Sammy but I guess she must have talked to Sammy because she seemed to be pretty clued up as to what was going on. I could sense that she was trying hard to find some consolation for me but she wasn't succeeding. Yet I needed an audience because I felt that I was letting the whole thing collapse and I knew there was nothing I could do. I had to call it a day, and on my own I couldn't have done this. I'd just have got sadder each day till it was just a shambles, and I'd have taken away a chunk of Sammy's assurance.

On the fourth evening Sammy had an appointment and

we agreed to meet for lunch the next day. When I came back from dinner that was a knock on the door and when I called out it was the faithful Miss Kujawska. I saw her look at the pile of butts in the ashtray. She went over to the sideboard and came back with a glass of whisky. I smiled. 'The Englishman's emotional medicine.'

'The Russian's too, except that it's generally vodka.'

We both sat down and the only difference was that I needed to sit down. She was wearing a pale blue light denim trouser suit. A sort of Chairman Mao affair except that it looked very elegant. She was watching me drink the whisky and she put her hands in the jacket pockets as if to give them something to do.

And then she said, 'Do you want to talk to me about it?'

I shook my head because I couldn't speak and instantly she put her hand on mine and said, 'I know it must be terrible but don't be unhappy or Sammy will be unhappy too. Even if you don't end up together she needs to know she's got a father and to know that he's strong. You can't do more for her.' Then I turned and looked at her face. She was so beautiful and she wasn't coy like a western woman. She just let me look and watched me looking and, although I cursed myself for my stupidity, I said, 'You said the first evening we talked that you cared about me. Did you really mean that?'

She spoke in almost a whisper, 'Yes, I meant it. I really care about you.'

'Why?'

'Because you're not like other men I've known. Because of the files I've read, I know more about you than most wives ever know about their husbands, and although there are some things there that I don't like, I feel you are a good man and a loving man. I don't think you've been happy for a long time and I think it's a great shame that you were brought back into counter-intelligence, and I'm sad that because of your love of your daughter you have had to leave your own country and I'm sad that because of your daughter you are going to get hurt again.'

134

I reached out and took her other hand, the hand with the ring on it. 'Are you engaged?'

'What does that mean, engaged?'

'Are you engaged to be married, are you betrothed?'

She shook her head. 'No, why do you ask?'

'Because you are wearing a ring on the third finger of your left hand and in my country that means you are engaged.'

'No, I'm not engaged and in Poland we wear wedding rings and rings for being engaged on our right hands anyway.'

Most women would have feigned ignorance of the point of my question and would have gone on to ask me why I asked. I felt she knew, and had pleasure in her honesty. I looked away and said, 'Can I ask you one other question?'

'About Sammy?'

'No, about you.'

'Of course.'

I realized that my voice was very flat with fear when I said, 'On the card on my bedside table you wrote, "Love Grazyna" – did you mean that?'

She nodded, 'Yes.'

'Really mean that?'

She nodded. Then my arms were round her and my lips were on hers and one of her hands was stroking my neck. After a long time we were looking at each other again and I said, 'I think I must have cared about you from the moment I saw you.'

She laughed, 'You didn't look like you cared. You looked very lonely, a bit angry and very defensive.'

I grinned. 'That was the colonels, not you,' and I kissed her again and then still holding her hand I said, 'What the hell are we going to do.'

She leaned back in the chair and looked up at the ceiling. 'What do you want to do?'

'I want to be with you.'

She nodded but said nothing although she knew that wasn't an answer, and I knew it wasn't an answer too, and was coward enough to pat the ball back to her. 'Where do you want us to be?'

Still with her head against the back of the chair she turned and looked at me and said, 'Wherever you want us to be.'

'You mean Egypt, Cuba, the Argentine – or Poland.'

Her soft lips trembled. 'No, I mean wherever you want us to be – you'll have to learn to trust me.'

When someone you know you love has just told you that they love you without you saying your piece first, there's about a minute when all the world is still, as if some giant bomb has exploded and the bits haven't started to fall. Your love has no history – no pains and no pleasures, no names of other men to haunt you, but if you're forty-eight you know that disentangling a life and making a new one is going to be difficult and perhaps painful for both of you. I felt a need to test the temperature of the water; a need to find out the areas about which I should have to worry in future. I knew she was still looking at me and I leaned over so that our faces were close together.

'Grazyna, I love you. Will you marry me?'

The hazel eyes were steady on mine. The long black eyelashes had no coy flutter and there was no obliging smile. She just said very softly, 'Of course.' There were no conditions, no ifs or buts.

'What about your life, your friends, your job and all that?'

I felt ashamed when she said, 'My parents are both dead, I have very few friends and my job is just a job. They all stopped mattering when you first kissed me.'

'Why?'

'When I first saw you your confidence must have been at its very lowest, but I could tell that although you loathed what you had been forced to do, you hadn't taken long to make up your mind to do it. And although you were the loser, you seemed to me a better man, a bigger man than your new masters. You seemed like a man who's made up his mind about what he is, and how he wants to be. I felt then I'd be safe with you.'

Like any man would be, I was pleased with this analysis

and tempted enough to throw the dice again.

'You said I'd have to learn to trust you, and it's not meant as an insult when I say I can't. It's got nothing to do with my feelings. It's just simple, boring old reflexes. They spent years building suspicion on to a reasonably alert mind, and at the end of six years I didn't need to be suspicious, I just knew when people were telling lies before they had made up their minds to try it on. It's both less, and more, than suspicion; it's knowing – a kind of telepathy. Women have it about men they love and I had it about everybody.

'Then when I was a civilian I had to try and forget all this and, of course, you can't do that. So it means that you try not to hear the lies because it doesn't seem fair. But you haven't pretended with me so I won't pretend with you. As an intelligence agent, I bear in mind that you are Polish, probably communist, probably employed by the KGB and this whole thing could be set up by them.' There were tears stacked up along her lower eyelid and, when I said the last bit they overflowed, but I kept on, 'And as a man I mistrust because I am very much older than you. I cannot think what I have to offer you. You're beautiful, and I can't believe my luck has changed so late in life.'

There was no lace-handkerchief, just a good substantial Polish sniff and a slight tremble of the lower lip that reminded me of Sammy when I said 'no more stories', and even then I was always good for one more.

'Well,' she said, 'dealing with the intelligence agent first. I am Polish, that's true, but I'm a woman and that's more important. And I'm not a communist for the same reason that you are not a capitalist – I don't really care one way or the other – I'd prefer to be left alone. I don't work for the KGB but I do work for the Polish Secret Police, the PZPR, and I suppose to you that's virtually the same. According to your records, you've worked for MI5, SOE and now you're working for SIS, but I don't think you said you loved me as part of a plot. I understand you thinking that this could be a frame-up but there wouldn't by any point. You're here already, you're out of action, so whether you love me or not won't help the KGB or the PZPR. It will probably just make life difficult for both of us. At best, they'll leave us alone, at worst, they'll try to abuse our love.

'Your suspicions as a man are a bit mixed. You didn't disbelieve me when I said that Sammy loved Yuri and there's almost exactly the same difference between our ages as between theirs. For me, I love you, and your age and the colour of your eyes have nothing to do with it.'

'If Sammy wants to stay in Poland, would you come back with me to England?'

'They'd never let us go.'

I laughed, 'I didn't propose asking them.'

Her face was drained of colour. 'They'd kill us if they caught us – if we were lucky.'

I nodded. 'So how do you answer my question?'

'There's a piece in the Bible that I'd always liked very much, it says, "Wither thou goest, I will go".'

I held both her hands in mine and looked at her very intently. 'You really do mean that.'

She kissed me on the mouth. 'I love you and I'll never say anything I don't mean – I mean it.'

'And if I can persuade Sammy to leave Poland and go to one of the specified countries, you'd go there too?'

She gently shook her head. 'It's going to take you a long time to learn, but you'll have to get used to it. I'll go wherever you want.'

'Do you mind of it takes a few days to sort out the situation with Sammy?'

'Of course not.'

It was two o'clock in the morning and it seemed perfectly normal and natural that at three o'clock in the morning, as my hand was reaching to put out the bedside lamp, I should be looking down at that small head on my shoulder, with its mass of long black hair; and that one beautiful leg was lying across both of mine.

CHAPTER TWENTY-FOUR

The next morning it was hard to believe there was ever snow in Poland because the sun was battering its way through the venetian blinds. For one minute I'd been terribly unhappy because Grazyna was gone, but on the coffee table at the side of the bed was a white rose, a picture postcard of the Chopin statue in Lazienki Park, with a message on the other side which said, 'Dearest Edward, I love you and always will. Have a good time with Sammy. I'll be waiting for you whatever time you get back. Your Grazyna.'

I got to the Bristol a little early, but Sammy was already there. She was sitting in the rather old-fashioned lounge on a big plush sofa. She wore a dress of what looked to me to be silk with a pattern of big roses over it. It was very old-fashioned and very beautiful. I looked to see if there was a ring on her hands but there was nothing. Once again a pretty girl patted a seat beside her and before I sat down I leaned over and kissed her.

There were a number of Polish army officers who cast interested glances her way but she was quite oblivious to the interest she aroused. She chatted for five minutes about the weather, about a walk she'd taken that morning and the difficulty of getting fresh milk, and I knew that this was her way of not talking about our situation. I felt it would be kindest to lead up to it my own way and interrupted her by saying, 'How do you say "I love you" in Polish?' and with a slight frown, she said, 'Ja ciebie kocham.'

I asked her to write it down for me, and I practised it several times till in the end she laughed and said, 'Don't improve it any more or you'll sound like a routine Pole and the touch of English accent makes it sound far more attractive,' and apropos nothing at all, she re-arranged my tie and tightened the knot as any good wife would and then the penny fell and with one hand on my shoulder she said, 'I've just realized why you want to be able to say "Ja ciebie kocham." It's because of Grazyna, isn't it?'

'What makes you say that?'

'Well, I wouldn't have thought of it if you hadn't asked how to say I love you. Then I suddenly realized how alike you two are. You'll be a good pair.'

'You mean I would enjoy having an *affaire* with her.'

She smiled. 'No, not at all. She's not an *affaire* kind of girl and you're not an *affaire* kind of man.'

'How do you know?'

'I just do. I'm pretty, so I know a lot about men. I can smell the phonies a mile off and I'd bet my last rouble that you're a one-girl man.'

I laughed. 'There's a song called "Samantha" that talks about a "one-gal guy".'

'Yes, my dear Poppa, the film was called *High Society*, Bing Crosby sang the song not much helped by Grace Kelly and there was another version of the film called *Philadelphia Story*.'

'Touché, I ought to have remembered I was talking to a leading light of the film industry. Are you a one-man gal?'

The smile went and she was serious. 'Grazyna told me that you'd asked about Yuri and that she'd told you about us. Do you mind?'

'No, of course not.'

'I was going to tell you anyway. I was selfish to ask you about staying in Poland anyway.'

'Did Grazyna say anything else?'

'Nothing important anyway, but I got the impression that she knew that you didn't want to stay in Poland and now I come to think of it, I can remember her asking me to be very gentle with you.'

'Tell me about Yuri. What sort of a man is he?'

She blushed. 'I can say what all girls say to their fathers. I love him and he loves me. He's gentle and kind and clever. I trust him and nobody else interests me.'

'Are you going to marry him?'

'Well, if we stay in Poland, and we are neither of us

140

particularly anxious to go back to Moscow, we plan to get married, but if we do have to go back to Moscow we may have to wait a year or so for political reasons. In Poland, just living together is rather frowned upon and, in any case, we both rather like the idea of being married.'

We had our meal brought to us in the lounge and although I knew this was probably the last time I'd see her, I didn't feel sad because she was happy, self-confident and obviously capable. So when the meal was over, I said, 'It's been a surprise seeing you after all these years.'

'Why?'

'I think you're a lot like me and what you need much more, and what you've got, is Yuri's love. You've got a job, you've obviously got a bright mind and, although I couldn't stick living in a communist country, I think you're used to it and I don't want to disturb what you've got.'

There were tears in the blue eyes this time, 'Is this a disappointment to you, Dadda?'

'Well, I suppose in a way it is but I'll make arrangements that wherever I am you can always get in touch with me if you need me or even if you don't.'

She looked worried. 'And what are you going to do? Where are you going to with Grazyna?'

I smiled at her but knew I couldn't tell her, so I said. 'Oh somewhere where there's some sunshine. I'm not very fussy. How about we go for a walk in Lazienki Park again?'

She said very quietly, 'That would be lovely,' and I knew she knew that that was where we were going to say goodbye.

We sat for an hour on the same park bench by the Chopin statue and at the end of that time we kissed more like lovers than father and daughter and then with her hands in mine, she said, 'Don't forget to say it properly. It's "Ja ciebie kocham" and remember that there are two girls who love you almost the same way,' and with that she was gone and I watched my daughter walk away, till she was just a pretty young woman ducking under willow trees that hung over the path and waving till she was out of sight.

I sat on the bench on my own for nearly twenty minutes, trying to think about what I'd done and what I'd got to do and then I walked back to the hotel.

I didn't go back to my room. I knocked on Grazyna's door which opened immediately and there she was, all five foot five of her, and she held up her mouth to be kissed and her eyes were closed, and I looked down on the gentle face and without kissing her I said, 'Ja ciebie kocham,' and the big eyes came open and she said, 'It sounds lovely when you say it. How did you learn it?'

'From Sammy,' and then I kissed her and went inside her room. It was much smaller than mine and the furniture and décor were modern. It was rather like good-class servant's quarters attached to the tycoon's suite. I put my finger to my mouth as a warning to her and said, 'I've just been to the park again with Sammy. How about we go, too?'

She responded easily and I signalled to her to take her coat and her handbag. When we were outside in the corridor I said, 'Can you walk a long way in those shoes?' She nodded. I went back into my own room and picked up my shaving kit and left everything else. Nobody stopped us as we went out, and as we got into the Ulica Krucza we held hands and I said, 'Let's go somewhere we can talk.' She hailed a taxi and ten minutes later we got off at a bridge by a river. From the traffic on the river, I realized it must be a pretty important highway, which meant it must be the Vistula.

'Is this the Vistula, Grazyna?'

'No, this is the Wisla.'

I laughed. 'I guess they're one and the same,' but she went all Polish and said, 'What a silly translation. They don't sound anywhere near the same.'

I smiled down at her. 'Let's not start our married life arguing about rivers of Poland,' and her hand came up and stroked my cheek and a few minutes later we were sitting on the river bank and I felt it was time to start the sermon.

'Do you still want to be with me, Grazyna?'

'Yes, of course.'

'Well, if you do it means that we're not going back to the

hotel. Right at this minute we're on the run and every minute's going to count. If they catch us, at the best we'll end up in a labour camp in the Soviet Union, at worst, we'll both be killed. Whatever happens I want to be with you and this means that we could stay in Poland, or we could go to one of the countries they designated for Sammy and me and there would be no trouble for either of us. They'd see you as a piece of insurance to keep me out of their way and out of mischief. But I don't want to do this. First of all I'd have no dignity so I'd only be half a man, and secondly I couldn't stick living by courtesy of the KGB. I have been a capitalist hyena for too many years and I have been in the spy business for too many years not to know what communism is all about. There's a lot I don't like about the West but there's nothing at all I like about communist Russia, except Rostropovich, Pasternak, Solzhenitsyn and a few more creative people.'

She put her small hand over my mouth. 'You don't have to justify and you don't have to explain. There's a lot you don't know that I could tell you, but none of it matters and nothing matters to me except you, and our being together. You're the boss, so what do we do?'

'We're going to need money, shelter, transport and a map. I've got about twenty-two English pounds. How much will I get for these on the black market?'

'About nine thousand zloty.'

'Is that a lot of money, or nothing?'

'Well, it's about what I earn in six months.'

'Do you know how to change it on the black market?'

'Yes, I can do that easily but we'd have to go back into the centre of town to do it.'

'Can you get me a map – a school atlas would do.'

'Yes, I can get that at the CDT but it won't be very detailed.'

'That doesn't matter. I just want roads and railways and rivers.'

I opened my wallet and gave her all my money. 'You'll have to go on your own, Grazyna. I'm too obvious; English clothes, English haircut. I'd be far too easy to pick out. I'll wait for you here. Don't be longer than you can help.'

She looked at her wrist-watch. 'Expect me back in about an hour and a half.'

About half an hour after she'd gone, the sun began to set behind me and it was quite chilly. I wished I'd thought to ask her to get me an overcoat. It would cover up my English clothes and I was going to need one to keep warm. After another half-hour, I was really cold; there was a mist rising from the river bank and I felt terribly depressed. I'd so looked forward to seeing Sammy and making a new life with her and our time together had been terribly short and I'd now probably seen her for the last time. Was I stupid to accept the position and not insist that we went away together? Was she really going to be happy? At eighteen, did she know what she was doing? What sort of father gives up so easily. It's all very well to adopt an easy-going attitude but maybe fathers were better fathers if they laid down the law and did what they thought was right. How much had I turned a blind eye to my daughter because I had the prize of Grazyna's love to fall back on? How much was I suiting myself and letting Sammy carry out some foolish whim? I had no idea at all how to get out of Poland and even if I succeeded I'd probably get thirty years when I got back to England. 'The firm' didn't like traitors and they wouldn't count my feelings for Sammy as any kind of an excuse.

After two hours I was desperate to see Grazyna. It was nothing to do with escaping; it was just that I needed my twenty-four-year-old mother and the security that she gave me. There were anglers with lines on the bank and lovers walked on the pathway behind me. The whole world had something to do that evening but I was waiting for a girl who I was sure had by now been caught.

It was almost three hours after she'd gone when a figure on the pathway turned down towards me and there she was. I was almost angry at the delay as if it was her fault. As I opened my mouth to say something harsh, she said, 'I'm sorry I've been so long. You must be terribly worried, but I had difficulty in changing the money because one of the "stilyagi" recognized me and I had to go across to another

144

part of town because they thought I was trying to trap them for the PZPR. Then I decided to buy you a coat because I felt you'd be cold tonight and I've also bought a torch. It was easy to buy the torch but it took me ages to find a shop with batteries.'

Her coat was very Russian with a little white fur collar and, pleased by the weight and warmth of a Polish overcoat that felt as if it was made out of army blankets, I kissed her and felt like something out of *Dr Zhivago;* but there wasn't any snow and there wasn't a fifty-piece orchestra sawing away in the background and the bottoms of my trousers were wet and I'd never liked that since Magdeburg.

We walked along towards the main road to Warsaw and sat in the shelter of the archway of the bridge, and as I looked at the two-page spread of the map of Poland I felt a bit like Eisenhower planning D-day. She put an arm round me and rested her chin on my shoulder to look at the atlas with me, and a long capable finger pointed out a large blob and said, 'That's Warsaw.'

'Yes, I know, sweetie.'

She laughed. 'I love it when you call me sweetie. It's a beautiful name.'

'Well, it's not actually a name but if our first child is a girl I promise you we'll call her Sweetie.'

'Well, whatever it is, I like it.'

'Good, now we'd better get on and look at this map and I've got to tell you that there's something terribly wrong with Poland. Just look at this,' and I pointed with my finger. 'Practically every railway, every river and most of the roads go from north to south. There's almost nothing going from east to west. Now, where would you make for if you had to decide?'

'The obvious places to make for are Stettin, Danzig or Berlin – I'm assuming that we're going to England.'

'Yes, that's what I'd got in mind but I really do want to please you too. So tell me what you think.'

'Like I said, I'll do whatever you say.' She looked at me very lovingly.

'Well, you said Stettin, Danzig or Berlin were the obvious

places to go to so in my book that eliminates them straight away. I think what we've got to do is head for East Germany but not for Berlin. You can take it for granted that as soon as they've discovered we've gone they'll alert all the ports and they'll stake out all the important railway stations, particularly the junctions, but they'll give far more attention to the roads because that's the easiest way of getting to the west. Also, they know as well as I do that a car gives you a hell of a lot more chance of evading traps and surveillance than trains or boats ever do.

'So I think they're going to put their money on Danzig, Stettin and the roads to the west. Now if you look on the map here you'll see that the railway heading west goes to Lodz where the line from the south-east from Jaroslaw and Ostrowiec joins it. So we've got to get west to the other side of Lodz to avoid the junction. We could go straight on once we'd got a train to Cottbus in East Germany and then to Leipzig; but it would be dead easy to cover every train for weeks crossing the East German border so we'll head down here to this place Glogow and then on foot or by road transport and go over the East German frontier at Gorlitz. After that we'll head for Magdeburg.'

She said quietly, 'Wasn't it in Magdeburg that you were interrogated by the NKVD?'

'Yes, it was, but that doesn't matter. It's good familiar territory as far as I'm concerned. How much money did you get on the black market?' She fished in her handbag and brought out a thick packet of notes. 'Here's 30,000 zloty.'

'But I thought you said we'd get about 9,000.'

'Well, I sold my wrist-watch so that we'd have more money.'

'But that just wasn't necessary. It was a beautiful watch and it was yours.'

'It wasn't mine, it was ours and it was necessary.'

'Why?'

'They already know we've gone.'

'How the hell do you know that. We've only been gone a few hours.'

'It's nearly eleven o'clock. You left the hotel before noon and you've only been back for ten minutes. I saw you slip your razor in your pocket and that will be the first thing they'll look for in your room. We've both been away from the hotel together for about five hours. They've had no report from me. The telephone won't be answered in either room and I'm afraid that's going to be enough.'

'But that's just guesswork, they're not that bright.'

'I'm afraid you're wrong. There was an announcement on the nine o'clock news. I heard it in the shop when I was buying your coat.'

'What did it say?'

'It said that a captured English spy had escaped with a Polish–German girl. The police, transport authorities, hotel managers, shopkeepers were warned to keep a look out for them and report any suspicious foreigners to the police. It said the English spy was armed and dangerous and it gave a reasonable description of us both.'

'Are you Polish–German?'

'No, I'm Polish–Polish.'

'Well, they must know that. Why the hell do they put the German bit in?'

'Well, the Poles aren't too fond of the Germans as you can imagine, and if you say somebody's Polish–German it implies that their mother probably fraternized with the Germans and it's going to give everybody a good incentive. Nothing to do with politics; you get your own back on the Germans and feel patriotic and self-righteous at the same time. They didn't give either of our names but that's pretty well standard policy so that if they don't get us they don't lose face, and they can still claim an outstanding success and cook up some story as to how the couple was shot trying to get over some frontier or out of some port.'

By two in the morning she was trembling violently from the cold and my mind was numb. I just couldn't think. I tried to make my brain work but it had had too much to do and it was on strike so I gave up thinking. There's something strange about our thought processes. You can't think a good thought because you want to. I don't even know how

147

I think. The thoughts just come from some layer of mind and memory and I feel I just supply the machinery because the thoughts are often as much a surprise to me as to anyone else. Maybe that's what Joan of Arc's voices were all about.

As I sat there dull and clobbered, I had an idea. 'Do you know of any CIA men in Warsaw?'

She thought for quite a time, then said, 'I know of a man who's suspected of being a CIA man. He came here after the war from America – Philadelphia, I think. I think his name is Grabowski and he speaks Polish fluently but with an American accent. I think he also speaks fluent German. His mother and father who were both from Lodz went to America just before the war. I'm not sure whether he went with them or joined them later. The PZPR have suspected him for some time but I think they aren't sure who he works for: it might be the CIA or one of the West German organizations like the one that Gehlen runs.'

'What sort of a job has he got?'

'Oh, he just hangs around foreign journalists, and acts as chauffeur or guide or adviser. Whatever they want, he'll do it.'

'Do you think he's on the phone?'

'I should think he would be else they wouldn't be able to contact him at short notice.'

'How far are we from the nearest phone box?'

'It's on the Wisla side of the main road, just by where the taxi dropped us.'

It took us twenty minutes to reach there, and when we were inside the kiosk there was no directory so I asked her to check his number with the exchange. After five minutes and a pack of lies, we got it, and all we had to do was dial, but there was just one small difficulty. What the hell do you say to a strange man at half past two in the morning to find out if he works for the CIA. I decided that it was best not to talk to him in English and opted to try him out in German.

Grazyna dialled the number and I heard it ringing at the other end. It was several minutes before anyone answered

148

and then a very decisive voice said, 'Grabowski mowi, kto to jest?'

'Ich möchte Herr Grabowski, bitte.'

'Wer ist das?'

'Ich brauche Ihre Hilfe.'

'Was für Hilfe?'

'Beratung.'

Once he grasped that the kind of help we wanted was advice, he seemed to settle down, but when I told him that I didn't want the advice over the phone but in person and right now, he was both suspicious and mercenary.

'Look friend,' he said, 'my advice isn't cheap, and at three o'clock in the morning it will cost you a packet.'

'It's O.K., Mr Grabowski, you'll be paid.'

'Fair enough,' he said. 'You'd better come round right now.'

'I'm afraid that won't be possible. You'll have to come to us.'

The suspicion was back in his voice again. 'If I have to come out to you it's going to cost you extra. Where are you anyway?'

'We're at the main road bridge over the Wisla.'

'Where are you? In a house, or what?'

'We'll stay near the telephone kiosk.'

'What do you look like? You'd better give me some sort of description.'

'That won't be necessary, Mr Grabowski, we'll be looking out for you and I'll expect you to say to me the first few lines of the Lord's Prayer in English.'

He was very cautious then and I could hear the voice harden when he said, 'What the hell. Is this some sort of ...' but at that point I hung up on him. I reckoned, knowing his kind, that both his greed and his curiosity would bring him out. These sort of men were the hangers-on of the intelligence game. Starting off on one side, getting caught and being turned, then graduating to being double agents and finally everybody loses count as to who is paying the extra fifty dollars a month. Then there's no retainer from anybody, just payment by results. They didn't make a

149

bad living but the living didn't always last very long, so while they were alive they were pretty nippy on their feet.

Grazyna and I leaned against the back of the telephone box and I smoked a cigarette. Less than fifteen minutes later, a small black Warszawa car came slowly down past the kiosk and when we moved out from behind, it stopped. The occupant made no hurry to get out and I made no move to cross over the road. It was nearly ten minutes before a man got out of the car, put his hands in his pockets and slowly walked towards the telephone kiosk. When he got near to us he was obviously surprised to see a girl as well as a man. He shook a cigarette from a packet, took out a lighter very slowly and lit the cigarette, and during that time he didn't take his eyes off my face.

When he blew out the first smoke, he said quite clearly, 'Vater unser, der Du bist im Himmel, heilig sei Dein Name,' and I didn't say a word because he was trying me out for size.

Two more drags at the cigarette and he said quickly, 'Our Father, which art in Heaven, hallowed be Thy name.'

Maybe he didn't know any more but he left it at that and so did I. He was what I expected and we didn't need the fancy stuff of misters any more so I said, 'Grabowski?'

'Henryk Grabowski. Who are you and who's the doll?'

'She's not a doll, Grabowski, she's a lady and who she is is none of your business. I want your advice, maybe some help, and if I find it satisfactory you'll be paid.'

'What are you offering?'

'I'm not offering anything. If we just take your advice we'll pay you 10,000 zloty. If we need your help, you'll be paid 10,000 dollars, or any other currency you name.'

'Let's go to the car.'

Grazyna and I piled into the back seat which was pretty cramped. 'Have you got anywhere we can go and talk, Grabowski, and we don't mean your place.'

'Sure.'

'Where is it?'

'I've got another room in Ulica Bolecha.'

I looked at Grazyna and she nodded, and I said in English, 'O.K., let's go.'

He turned round in his seat and had a good look at me and he said slowly in German, 'Sind Sie Auslandsdeutsch,' and with those few words I reckoned I'd got him placed. His hair ought to be as grey as mine and I didn't have much doubt that he'd served in one of the Polish traitor units with the Wehrmacht. Auslandsdeutsch was a good old German word that only a Nazi would use, coined by Goebbels. It aptly described Germans living outside the main frontiers of Germany. Those poor souls who always seemed to be suffering persecution in some neighbouring democracy that gave the Führer a good excuse for authorizing an invasion. Austria, Czechoslovakia, Danzig and so on, all had their population of Auslandsdeutsche who were longing to return to the Fatherland and if they couldn't get to the Fatherland, the Fatherland could come to them.

'No, I'm not German, Grabowski.'

'I'd have guessed from your accent you started somewhere near Hanover.'

'A good guess but you'd still have been wrong.'

'I'd put your English accent somewhere round about Manchester.'

'Look friend, I love playing "Twenty Questions" but not at this time of day so let's get to your place and we'll continue the guessing games there.'

It was only another five minutes before we turned into a narrow street of old buildings and the car stopped alongside a row of what must have been workers' cottages. They were still clean and neat and Grabowski sorted through his keys to let us in one of the middle ones. The same key gave us entrance to the first room on the right. It was small with two armchairs and a double bed, a wardrobe, a chest of drawers and it reeked of cheap perfume. There was an engraving of some battle scene with Polish cavalry officers brandishing swords and wearing Shakos at rather rakish angles. There were standard photographs on the wall of Gomulka and Ulbricht, and a quite pretty blonde in a wedding gown smiling into the camera on the arm of the SS officer. If you added that little lot to the tatty doll on the

151

bed, of the kind that's given away at third-rate night clubs, you didn't need much imagination to obtain a picture of the owner. Whoever it was, it wasn't Grabowski, but he was obviously at home and he motioned us to sit wherever we wanted.

We both sat on the bed and we must have looked a bit like Hansel and Gretel. Grabowski didn't have grey hair. It was very black and I'd have guessed that it wasn't dyed by a hairdresser but was a do-it-yourself job. The stubble round his chin was grey. He must have been handsome once with the kind of good looks that sold vacuum cleaners to lonely housewives. The kind of man who always had clean shirts and the latest fashion in suits, the kind who set trends in male cosmetics. A conqueror of waitresses and barmaids, and I knew he'd be verbally agile and would lie like a polecat, while the big blue eyes that didn't match his hair, gazed frankly into mine.

It was going to be easy, but with this kind of man you had to let them boost up their egos and then clobber them quickly because on the way down they would do as they were told. So when I asked him what he did for a living I took time out to think whilst he gave us the old, old story and I was only vaguely conscious of the scoops that he'd provided for the incompetent reporters from the world Press. One thing was very clear, he wanted that 10,000 dollars in a big way. I tried to listen to the bitter end but it was going to take too long so I finally interrupted him and said, 'Grabowski, are you interested in the 10,000 dollars?' and I got the full treatment of the pearly smile that would have launched a thousand Hoovers, and he made a weak man's attempts at playing it cagey. 'It depends on what sort of help you need, friend. I'm a pretty solid citizen and I've got a reputation to maintain but I'm sure we can do business.'

I smiled back and wished I'd cleaned my teeth in the last two days. 'How do I know I can trust you, Mr Grabowski?'

He liked getting back to the mister bit and, with palms apart and a look of pure frankness, he said, 'Ask me anything you want.'

'O.K., Grabowski, how about you take off your shirt.'

'Say, what the hell is this all about.'

I stared at him hard for a few moments. 'No shirt off, no 10,000 dollars, Grabowski.'

'Jesus,' he said, 'I thought I'd seen it all,' but he was sliding out of his jacket and undoing the clean white shirt. When it came off it exposed a white singlet, so looking at his face to see how long it would take before the penny dropped, I said 'Lift up your arms.' He grinned and lifted them up high. They'd been up for nearly thirty seconds before he got the point but it was time enough for me to have seen the little tattoo under his left armpit. It wasn't very big and if you tried to have it removed it left a tell-tale scar that was just as damning as the tattoo itself. The good old German mind hadn't wanted its élite in the SS to bleed to death for want of a supply of blood of the right group so they had tattooed the blood group number under the left armpit of every SS man. Which was great while they were winning but when it was all over it was mighty inconvenient. Before Grabowski could start the big indignation scene I said, 'O.K., Grabowski, now we can talk.'

He occupied himself with putting on his shirt and jacket and when he sat down he'd partially recovered, and just to maintain the status quo, I said, 'Which SS division were you with?'

'The Hermann Goering Division.'

'Fair enough, well let's bring your story up to date.'

He fiddled with his fancy cuff-links and leaned back in the chair.

'Have you got any contacts with the CIA?'

You could see the desire to be important and the fear of being trapped fighting it out on his face, and as I expected the need to be important won out. 'It's quite possible,' he said.

I stood up and pulled Grazyna to her feet with me. 'Look, Grabowski, it's about four in the morning, I'm very tired. I've got a lot to talk about and you will have a lot to do. If you haven't got links with the CIA, you're of no

153

interest to me and we're both wasting our time. This lady here used to work for the PZPR. In fact, she only finished with them today. She gave me your name as a suspected CIA man. As far as I am concerned, as long as you've got a contact with them that's for real we can do business.'

He motioned us back on to the bed and, trying very hard to look in charge of the situation, he crossed one leg over the other and said, 'I think we can talk business. What is it you want?'

'Where is your contact with the CIA?'

'In Frankfurt.'

'How do you contact them?'

'By radio.'

'What time do you go on net?'

'They've got a twenty-four hour listening post. I can go on any time but it takes me twenty minutes to get my set-up working.'

'What code do you use?'

'Number two diplomatic.'

'Is that changed every week, or what?'

'It changes twice a day at twelve o'clock Central European Time.'

'What's the change based on?'

'The third word of the first news item on the Voice of America newscast at nine every morning.'

'Who's your contact?'

'I don't have any contact at all.'

'How do you get your instructions?'

'I get them in writing.'

'What do you use for the post office.'

'The stuff's taped to the back of one of the cisterns in the lavatories at the Bristol.'

'How do you get paid?'

'By Americans coming to Warsaw. Generally journalists who know me, anyway.'

'How do you get paid? In dollars or zlotys?'

'I get paid in pounds but they also pay money into a Swiss bank account for me.'

'What's the number of the account?' Without any hesitation he said, '10350556.'

'What was your army number?'

'974659.'

There are only two multidigit numbers that a man ever remembers all through his life; one's his army number and the other is his Swiss bank account number – if he's got one. I was beginning to feel that Grabowski could help.

'What was the last piece of information that you sent through to Frankfurt and when did you send it?'

'I sent it at ten o'clock this evening and it was about a man and a girl who'd escaped,' and he stopped with his mouth open. 'For Chrissake, that must be you two. Look, I don't want anything more to do with it. Just get the hell out of here. I'll take you back to town and drop you anywhere you want.'

He was trembling and I let him tremble for a bit. 'If we get caught, Grabowski, they'll know we were here with you because we'll tell them and they'll be able to trace the telephone call and check this address. I can tell you that at the moment, although they suspect you, they're not sure who you work for. You probably work for anybody who'll pay you, but if you start messing about with me, you'll be finished. You won't work for anybody again, not even the journalists, and the PZPR will have you up against a wall before you can count ten; that little bit under your armpit will see to that.'

For a horrible moment I thought he was going to get down on his hands and knees but he managed to restrain himself. He was trembling violently now. He was happy playing the jackel but he didn't like getting mixed up with the lions, but trembling men are not much help so I felt it was time to dust him down and set him up again.

'How'd you like to get out of Poland, Grabowski?'

He half smiled. 'I wouldn't stand a chance.'

I looked at him like a father and he must have been a couple of years younger than me. 'If you do what I tell you to do and stick exactly to my instructions, I'll see that you go to any country you want. I'll see that you get a job and we'll probably raise more than the 10,000 dollars for you,

155

but I want to warn you, you've got to do exactly what I say, and if you start playing games or taking out any insurance, you've had it. So do you want to play?'

He hadn't got the courage to say yes out loud but he nodded his head vigorously.

'Right, I want you to get on to your contact at Frankfurt and give them a message. I'll dictate it to you now if you'll get a pencil and some paper.'

He picked up a copy of *Trybuna Luda* and taking out a pencil he held it poised over one of the margins and I dictated. 'Ted Bailey wants to report on Berger situation to CIA London care of Uncle Joe. Also requests assistance returned three bodies to Ebury Street.'

He looked up. 'Is that all?'

I nodded back to him but he wasn't going to let well alone.

'Will they understand what it's all about?'

I grinned at him. 'Let's try, shall we? Is it safe to stay on here and how long before you can get back to us?'

He had all the finesse of a seaside landlady when he said, 'Yes, you could stay here all right but I'll have to square up with the owner.'

I took out my wallet and gave him ten one-thousand zloty notes which he counted twice and then tucked into his hip pocket. 'I'll be back in two to three hours. You're entitled to help yourself to food and coffee. My friend won't mind,' and he stood there as if he were waiting permission to go, so I nodded and said very casually, 'If you're not back in three hours, we'll phone the PZPR before we leave.'

He shook his head. 'There'll be no need to do that, I'll be back.'

CHAPTER TWENTY-FIVE

Grazyna made us both a cup of coffee and we had two slices of bread each. It wasn't quite black but it wasn't quite brown either, and when I screwed up my face, Grazyna said, 'Don't worry, it doesn't taste very nice but it won't do you any harm.' I hated being in this stinking little room with her. She was so out of place, but we were going to be stuck there for some hours and I knew that we might as well make the best of it, so I said, 'You lie on top of the bed and get to sleep and I'll sleep on the armchair.'

She put her arm round my neck and said, 'Let's both sleep on the bed.'

I gave her a long kiss and patted her bottom. 'You know as well as I do that if we both get on the bed neither of us will get to sleep and we're going to need all the sleep we can get in the next few days.'

She stroked my cheek. 'That's better, Major Bailey, and I suppose I'd better do what you say,' and two minutes later, one passionate lover was sound asleep. I felt a bit like Horatio guarding the bridge. I'm afraid if it had been left to me the bridge would have been lost in five minutes and when the telephone rang it took what seemed to be hours to crawl out of the ground and I'd almost picked it up to answer it before I'd come to my senses.

Grazyna was snoring good lusty Polish snores, but the big, soft, gentle mouth still looked attractive and I kissed her awake and finally gave up and shook her awake.

'The phone,' I said, 'I don't know who it is. We'll have to play it by ear but speak in Polish.'

She had quite a conversation for about three minutes and then, as if I wasn't there, she lay down on the bed and went to sleep again. This time the shaking had some element of annoyance in it and when she woke the big beautiful eyes took one look at me and said, 'I love you so much,' and I said, 'Yes, I love you too, but what about the telephone call? Who was it? What did they say?'

She frowned. 'What ... oh yes, the telephone call. It was Grabowski. He wanted to make sure you didn't ring the PZPR. He's had some difficulties and he's on his way round. Is that all right?'

I nodded. 'Sounds great,' and with that she went off to sleep again.

It was about half an hour before the key turned in the lock and Grabowski came back. He looked very jaunty and rather self-important. He closed the door quietly and carefully and spoke in a whisper. 'I got your message through and I had to wait for them to come back with an answer. I've written it down here for you.' The message said 'Send basic report only on Berger operation Stop This required immediately Stop Assistance being arranged via big Pole from Waldorf Astoria Stop He will contact you via this network after your report Message ends.'

'Have you got any writing-paper, Grabowski?'

He fished out some fancy notepaper which was pale pink and stank of cheap perfume and he handed me a pen. In case I hadn't noticed, he said proudly, 'Parker 52.'

'How long can you send for in one session?'

'Up to about eighty groups.'

'Groups of five?'

'Yes.'

I got Berger's activities over in seventy-two and used the last eight to ask for some proof of authenticity. When I gave it back to Grabowski, we went over it carefully three times and I was glad to see he couldn't understand what it was all about, but he was beginning to feel he was on the winning side after all.

He looked very much the eager-beaver when he said, 'I'll get right back and send this, but you'll have to be patient because if I've got to wait for a message to come back, it might take them some time to decipher this and if the reply is long, I'll have to work on that, but I'll be right back as soon as I can.' And then he fished around in his pocket and brought out a small bar of chocolate. 'That's for the girl,' he said.

'Grabowski,' I said, 'we're going to get on well together. Get going,' and he got.

I'd worked out that it was going to take at least three hours before Grabowski came back and when I lay alongside Grazyna on the bed I tentatively put my hand on her hip and contemplated turning her towards me, and whilst the small battle between the forces of passion and self-sacrifice went on in my mind, she settled the matter when she murmured, 'I was wondering how much longer you were going to take,' and the big generous mouth was on mine and I've never known three hours go so quickly.

Somebody was shaking me awake. It was Grabowski.

'Bailey, I've got the reply for you. For authenticity they said tell you hot chocolate. I don't know what that means but I suppose you do. They're fixing for somebody to come from the American Embassy and he's due to arrive here any minute. I gather he'll have a message for you and some instructions.'

I borrowed a towel from Grabowski and shaved while Grazyna slept on. From my experience with American embassies, their man was going to be young, handsome and efficient and, as far as I was concerned, if Grazyna's long black hair covered her face that suited me fine.

Then minutes later there was a knock at the door and Grabowski let in a middle-aged man who looked more as if he'd spent a lifetime chopping down trees and posing for Kodak advertisements in red lumberjack shirts than working in embassies. He shook hands with me in what I'm sure he thought was a friendly fashion. It was a bit like putting your hand in an old-fashioned mangle.

'Well, well, Mr Bailey,' he said, 'we gather you need some help,' and turning to our companion he said, 'I expect Mr Grabowski has got a few things he needs to do because we've been taking up a lot of his time and I guess he wouldn't mind leaving us for about twenty minutes while we have a little talk.'

Grabowski was obviously disappointed not to be in on the chat, but the authority of this man was unmistakable and as he went to the door he said, 'I'll be about half an hour before I'm back. You just go ahead.'

The American embassy man took the armchair, and as he sat down he nodded in the direction of Grazyna. He said, 'I suppose that's the young lady in the case,' and he sounded a bit like a private detective gathering evidence for a divorce.

'My name's McLaughlin, Tom McLaughlin, and we've got a message from London to give any help we can. The ambassador's not too keen on us getting mixed up in this but he's left me to do a bit of liaison with you and we've had clearance from Washington to do whatever our people in London ask us to do. But you realize that if anything goes wrong, we don't know what it's all about and we'll be giving every assistance to the Polish authorities short of loading the guns for them. We couldn't do much for one of our own boys. As you're not even one of our nationals, I can't do much more than ride around with messages for you.' He looked over at me on the bed to see how I took all this. 'I'm glad of any help you can give me, Mr McLaughlin.'

He was rolling his own cigarettes and he was one of those experts who do it with one hand.

'I guess I'd better call you Ted, and before we start, Ted, have you got anything that could prove your identity? Passport, letters, that sort of thing.'

I shook my head. 'I haven't got a thing, Tom, but the young lady on the bed was until yesterday employed by the Polish secret police. She was part of my reception committee and she can confirm that I'm Bailey. I expect you heard on the news that she's on the run with me and I'm taking her back to England with me.'

He raised his eyebrows. 'It's not going to be that easy, my boy. You're not going to be able to hop on a train with a ticket for London; and doing a bolt with a Polish national, especially when she's been part of the PZPR, has made the Polish boys pretty mad, and I gather the Russians are leaning on them like they haven't been leaned on for a long time. There have been demonstrations outside the British Embassy. All fixed, of course, but they've been able to

160

pack the whole area with cops and the word came over from Sir What's-his-name, your ambassador, that they weren't intending to compromise their position in any way. Putting it mildly, they weren't at all pleased. The ambassador's been called to the Foreign Ministry twice in the last ten hours, and if I tell you the first time was at three in the morning you can count on it that, as far as your fellows are concerned, you've got your backside out in the snow.

'Anyway, let's not dwell upon these more formal aspects. I'm here to help. I gather you know one of our boys in London named Bill Autenowski and they're sending him across here to get you out. With a name like that, you won't be surprised if I tell you he's originally a Pole. They're not too happy about your young lady, and I doubt if they'll be able to extend any help to her. Even in your case...'

I interrupted him, 'Tom, I'll be glad if you'll tell them that if they don't include the girl they can forget the whole thing. Autenowski's wasting his time if he comes across here on any other basis than we go back together, and in addition to that I've promised Grabowski that he can jump on the wagon with us.'

Tom McLaughlin pursed his lips. 'Seems to me you've been a bit free with your promises, boy. I'd say you've got a bit of talking to do before they try and get *you* out and I can't see them giving a free lift to a couple of Polish nationals.'

He saw that I was about to explode and he put up both his hands. 'Now, first things first. How are you off for money?'

'We've got enough.'

'Is that pride speaking, fellow, or is that true?'

'It's true, we changed some pounds on the black market and my friend sold her watch.'

'Bill Autenowski has asked me to get you out of Warsaw,' he went on, 'and there will be a car coming for you tonight about eight o'clock. It's going to take you down to a little place called Gorlitz right near the Czech border. I've got some friends with a farm there and you and your young lady can have a couple of days' rest while Autenowski's getting over here. He'll be seeing me in Warsaw first and then I guess he'll be in touch with you.'

He looked me over and obviously found me wanting. 'I'll send some clothes round with the driver tonight, and if there's anything that you or the young lady want, my friends on the farm can fix that for you. You won't have to worry about money, we'll see to that.'

I went with him to the door and with a half salute he was gone. Grabowski was in the hallway smoking a cigarette, and I saw him get in the car with Tom McLaughlin.

CHAPTER TWENTY-SIX

It was nearly an hour before Grabowski came back. He was looking very pleased with himself. He handed me an envelope which had the official embassy seal on the back. It looked almost too important to open. The note inside was not addressed to anybody but it was obviously intended for me. It said WE'VE ARRANGED A DEAL WITH GRABOWSKI SO DON'T WORRY ABOUT HIM, HE'S HAPPY. AT EIGHT O'CLOCK THIS EVENING A VEHICLE WILL CALL FOR YOU AND THE GIRL. GRABOWSKI WILL BE GOING DOWN WITH YOU BUT HE WON'T BE STAYING. IF HE SHOWS SIGNS OF WANTING TO STAY TELL HIM TO GET THE HELL OUT OF IT. BEST OF LUCK.' I set fire to the note and the envelope, powdered the ashes in the grate, melted the seal and burnt two magazines so that if anybody tried analysing the ashes they'd have a lot of hard work and it would take a long time. When the ashes were powdered fine I slung on a jug of water. Not first-class security but the best I could do in the circumstances.

I stood up from the fireplace and said to Grabowski, 'I understand you've got a deal that satisfies you.'

He nodded eagerly like a child. 'Yes, Mr Bailey. I've made a good arrangement so you don't have to worry about me, and you can rest assured I'll look after you on the journey down tonight. The van will be here in about an hour so maybe you and your good lady would like to freshen up for the journey.'

I looked over his shoulder at Grazyna sitting on the bed, and she was grinning so it looked like her English was good enough to appreciate the rather gracious touch of being referred to as my 'good lady'.

It was five past eight when Grabowski heard the squeal of brakes and looking through a chink in the curtain said excitedly, 'It's here, it's here. We'd better go.'

He opened the door carefully but there was nobody about. It wasn't until we were out in the street that I realized my visions of a comfortable ride in a limousine were not to be. This was a farm lorry with a canvas hood and Grabowski, looking a bit apologetic, said, 'They say you and the girl have got to go in the back.' I hoisted Grazyna up and then clambered over the tail-board myself. The driver shone a torch through the driving-cab rear windows and it didn't look as bad as I'd expected. The back of the lorry was piled almost to the top of the canvas roof with bales of straw, but there was access to the front and immediately behind the driver's cab the bales were only two layers high and there was ample space for Grazyna and me to lie down.

I heard Grabowski call in a hoarse whisper, 'Are you all right,' and I said, 'Yes, we're fine but how long is the journey going to take?' and was staggered when he said, 'We'll be there by seven in the morning.' Although the straw was tightly baled it had been cut by hand and the stalks were long and comfortable to lie on and I thanked heaven that there weren't enough combines in Poland because there's nothing more uncomfortable than lying on bales of short cut straw.

Grazyna and I curled up together, and after a while she tried to work out where we'd got to but the last place she positively identified was the something-or-other cemetery which she told me was devoted to the graves of Russians who had died whilst liberating Poland. After that we were in open country.

I asked her if she knew what Gorlitz was like and she said, 'Well, that's the old German name for it. It used to be part of Saxony. It's on the river Neisse and was transferred to Poland in 1945 and now it's called Zgorzelice. I don't really know anything about it. It's got about a hundred thousand inhabitants, quite a bit of industry but it will be mainly farming.'

'Is there a PZPR office there?'

'Yes, there's quite a large one because it's so near the frontier. In fact it's near two frontiers, the Czech frontier and the GDR.'

'Do you know any of the people who operate there?'

'Yes, I know several of them and the top man is very good. His name is Jan Borowski. I think he worked for the German Abwehr during the war.'

'Would he know you by sight?'

She hesitated. 'I've met him at several conferences.'

     *   *   *

It was nearly two hours before we slept and when I awoke I was on my own. I called out, 'Grazyna, where are you?' and her voice came from above me.

'There's a hole in the hood,' she said, 'and I can see out. It's getting light and the last village we passed through is only about thirty kilometres from Zgorzelice.'

CHAPTER TWENTY-SEVEN

After about another twenty minutes we came off the main road. The truck jolted and bashed its way over the pot-holed surface of the twisting narrow roads and it was nearly another hour before it swung round and jolted to a stop. We waited for Grabowski because we could hear voices and, after a few moments, Grabowski appeared at the tail of the wagon and said, 'It's O.K. You can both get out.'

There was a man standing to one side as tall as me and as broad as me. His face, neck, arms and hands were tanned a deep brown. He stood in a manner that was both welcoming and proud.

He walked slowly over to Grazyna. With no manner of offensiveness he put his hand on her shoulder and turned her face to his. Looking at her intently, he said after a few moments, 'Well, my daughter, I hear you're going to marry the Englishman and that you've got difficulties in getting to the wedding. What's it all about?'

Grazyna had obviously forgotten our caution but her own dignity was enough. 'I think you know, sir, what our difficulties are.'

Before she could say more I turned to Grabowski and interrupted 'I should like us to be introduced before we talk further.'

Grabowski looked surprised. 'Sorry,' he said, 'Mr Bailey, Miss Grazyna Kujawska, this is Mr Tadeusz Czarny.'

Czarny turned to me and held out his hand. He had a good honest grip and I so liked this man immediately that I instinctively put both my hands round his.

'Mr Czarny, I know you'll understand if I say that till we know one another better, it would be safer for us all if you just discussed these things with me.'

His smile was warm and immediate. 'I'm a bad host, Mr Bailey. What will you think of us Poles. Come inside and have some coffee and some breakfast.'

He walked across the cobbled square and through a big open door in a beautiful but ramshackle old brick-built building that glowed red in the early-morning sunlight. He waved us to be seated around a big plain wooden table, and a few minutes later he had brought a steaming jug of coffee and a tray of cups and saucers. He told us to help ourselves and he sat down easily, drawing one of the kitchen chairs underneath him.

With both shirt-sleeved arms resting on the table he looked at me piercingly as if he was trying to assess what was in my mind. Then he leaned back and said, 'I think we are both old soldiers, Mr Bailey, so we don't need to play games with one another. I served in the RAF for four years. I didn't get on too well with the English but I admired them. They went to war for my country and we owe you what we can give. I have been asked to give you and the girl shelter and that, of course, I shall do. If you want it, you've got my friendship. So there we are.'

'That's very kind of you, Mr Czarny. I wondered how you spoke such good English. I'd better say that I don't know what we are supposed to do here or how long we are expected to stay, but I much appreciate your protection.'

He nodded, acknowledging this, and continuing the rather formal exchange said, 'I understand you and your lady will be here for two or three days at least, maybe even a week.' His eyes twinkled. 'As you know, we're a very moral lot, we Poles, but I've given you the best bedroom with a nice old-fashioned double bed, and while you're here I'll be glad if you will look upon it as a honeymoon. I've got a suit made in Poland that should fit you and when you walk about with the young lady, I suggest she talks quite a bit to you in Polish and there's no need for you to talk at all. You just nod as if you understand every word of it.' The eyes twinkled again. 'I'm sure Miss Kujawska will say the kind of things that any man would nod to.'

Seeing we had finished, our breakfast ended, he smacked his thigh. 'Now you two go upstairs. There's plenty of hot water. Have a good bath and get some real sleep and I'll wake you both about mid-afternoon. Then when you get up, I'll take you round the place to show you the layout. Your room looks out on the weir but I don't think the noise of the water will disturb you. My wife used to say that it's better than a sleeping draught.'

Grazyna said something in Polish and when Czarny replied he was speaking in Polish too. They spoke for quite a long time and all the while Czarny stared at the table. He didn't look up once. There were a few seconds' silence then Grazyna took my hand, and gently touching Czarny's shoulder as we passed, she led the way through a door and up an old wooden staircase; she might have lived there all her life. The bedroom was plain to the point of severity but spotlessly clean, furnished simply with beautiful carved wooden furniture that must have been several hundred years old, and the air that blew in through the open window smelt of mown grass from haymaking.

When the doors closed I said, 'What were you talking about?'

She told me that she'd asked where Czarny's wife was and he'd explained that the farm and the mill had belonged to her father, a German. That they'd only been able to hold on to it because of Czarny's war record coupled with the fact that he was a first-class farmer – and first-class farmers were in short supply. Falsely accused of collaboration with the Nazis about two years after Czarny had come home, his wife had been taken to the KGB headquarters at Poznan. Only after six months was she released and her treatment had been such that she died in great pain a few weeks later. He had told her a lot of other things, too, and it was quite clear that Czarny was a loner. He had scores to settle with the Russians and the Germans, and helping us was part of settling those scores.

It was nearly four o'clock before a knock on the door woke us both up, and when I called out 'Come in' it was Czarny himself who came in carrying tomatoes, a dark brown loaf and another big jug of coffee.

While we ate, he talked, sitting on the edge of the bed and for the first time his voice sounded young. 'This place

168

used to be called "Zwei Brücke Mühle" and now it's called "Mlyn dwóch mostów", which is the same thing in Polish. It's not really a mill, it's a farmhouse converted from a mill, but we still use the mill for grinding corn. The two bridges still exist over the river and because of the bend in the river they give the only easy access to the buildings. If you come in any other way, you've got at least a three-mile walk or drive on the road. So most of our visitors come over one or other of the bridges.

'I've got ten men working for me. This is a pretty large farm, about seven hundred acres. Four of the men I would trust with my life, three others I'm pretty sure about and three I wouldn't trust. The four I really trust already know about both of you, but they won't show any sign of it and I'm putting them to work on jobs that will have them near each of the two bridges so they'll act as a sort of forward patrol. Grabowski's gone and there's nothing that can connect you with this place, so I think you're going to be pretty safe, but I'm taking all the precautions I can. The farm is mainly arable – nearly five hundred acres of wheat or barley and the rest carries 150 Friesians. All the produce goes to the state. I get a decent salary and I don't starve. Farmers never do. Now let me show you round my place.'

It was over an hour later when we came back and because he talked in Polish all the time we were near the farmworkers, I went over some of the details with Grazyna and I drew myself a little map of the buildings and the outlying land that I could see from the upstairs windows. The buildings formed a rectangle with a big arched entrance where the roads from the two bridges converged. This was on the north side and the rest of that wall was an open shed for farm machinery. On the east side was the farmhouse itself which led into the mill building projecting over the river. There was a wooden bridge beside the mill, two planks wide with a single iron railing that crossed the river to the far side. The river then looped away from the farmhouse in both directions and flowed gently through soft water-meadows full of king cups and buttercups till half a mile further on in either direction it was straddled to

169

the north by the stone bridge with two arches and a more modern ugly iron bridge to the south.

The west side of the cobbled courtyard consisted of three cottages for farmworkers, and the south side was given over for half its length to a barn stacked high with straw and hay. The rest of its length was a milking parlour and a way out on to the main farm road which led past big fields with good grass keep where the Friesians were cropping it in three separate herds. It was just possible to see the first fields of wheat before the ground sloped away steeply about a mile from the buildings. Up the front of the main farmhouse there was a virginia creeper, ivy and honeysuckle and some small espaliered peach trees which were heavy with fruit. I had learnt a good deal about the farm and its owner that day and I planned to reconnoitre the two bridges, and the road the other side of the stream the next morning. After we'd had a good thick soup for supper, Grazyna and I went to bed.

Czarny, we had discovered, had flown a Hurricane in the Polish squadron. He had been a sergeant-pilot and had a DFM and bar. I liked him very much. He must have been a good man to be in a war with because he was single-minded. He must have been a good man to be in a fight with because he was brave. But I hoped we didn't give him any trouble because he wasn't the right material for dealing with the KGB or the PZPR. You needed to be an efficient coward like me to survive with them. My father had lost his life in the First World War, fighting to make a land fit for heroes to live in, and I'd fought in a war to make a land fit for cowards to live in because that gives us all a fair chance.

As we lay in bed the moon shone through the windows and it was all so peaceful with only the rushing of the water in the weir to emphasize the silence. We were soon asleep.

CHAPTER TWENTY-EIGHT

The noise of a car and the creaking of big gates woke me, and when I looked at my watch it was only two o'clock in the morning. I heard Czarny talking to someone downstairs. After he'd been talking for half an hour I woke up Grazyna and asked her to listen. All she could tell me was that she could hear odd words and that the stranger was talking in Polish but with a foreign accent. She couldn't tell what sort of accent; so few foreigners spoke Polish that she couldn't tell one accent from another.

I pulled on my trousers and my jacket and crept down the wooden stairs, and although he was talking in Polish the voice was unmistakable and to me the accent was unmistakable. It was American and beautiful and it was Bill Autenowski.

I opened the door and walked in and both men swung round quickly from the table where they were sitting. For a moment, Bill didn't recognize me in my genuine Polish gladrags and then the big, ugly face broke into a smile and it felt like Christmas Eve when he said, 'Hi, Ted, how're ya doing?'

I walked over and joined them at the table. 'Thanks for coming, Bill.'

The Pole stood up and said, 'I'll leave you two to talk together. You must have a lot to say.'

Some logs settled down on the fire and sparks flew up and we were on our own. I felt uneasy and I plunged straight in.

'I hope they got my message from McLaughlin that I'd come back with the girl and a safe conduct for her, or I don't come back at all.'

Bill looked down the table. 'Don't be so defensive, Ted. It won't pay you. Joe Steiner sends you all the best and the same from Jim Railton, and so that we don't get things

171

mixed up I'd better say that I've been seconded from the CIA to your lot for this operation so that everything that's being done is under orders from SIS, not from Washington.'

The big shoulders hunched up. 'London wants to know all there is to know about this Berger operation. So before we talk about you and how we get you out, you'd better put me in the picture.'

It took me two hours to tell him all I knew. At the end of that time he said, 'There are some points here that they'll need to know straight away so I need to get on the blower. I've a contact in Poznan.'

The telephone was an old-fashioned hook-on phone and Bill's Polish seemed to be adequate, but when he got through to whoever he was calling, the language they spoke certainly wasn't Polish. He talked for about ten minutes and some of the points he seemed to go over and over again, checking that they had been understood. When he finally hung up he was relaxed and smiling once more and he came back and sat with me at the table.

'You weren't speaking to your contact in Polish.'

Bill laughed and said, 'No. That was real genuine America,' and he laughed when he saw my disbelief. 'It was, Ted. One of the legacies of a mis-spent youth. I can get by quite happily in Navajo. There's a nice little Navajo Indian girl taking a course at Poznan University in biometry, by courtesy of the Soviet Union, and she helps us along from time to time.'

It was so American, so efficient, so crazy, I'd have liked to have known more, but Bill wasn't having any. 'Look, we'd better get down to your business. Are you really asking that we lift a Polish citizen, a full-blown member of the PZPR, illicitly out of Poland in defiance of the Polish government?'

'You know damn well I am. If it was a free country, it wouldn't be illicit. You don't give a damn for the Polish government any more than I do and if you don't mind me mentioning it we went to war for Poland, not because the Japanese bombed Portsmouth harbour. And while we were fighting on our own, you were taking all our realizable assets to supply us with arms to fight your war as well as ours.'

Most Americans would have either walked out or punched me on the nose because I meant what I said and I looked like I meant it, but there was more to this great big carcase than an ability to deal with spies and it would take more than a vinegary comment to wipe the smile off the big round face. He didn't even give me a dirty look, he just laughed. 'I gather from that little diatribe that what you're really saying is you love this girl.'

'Yes, I do,' I said quietly.

Bill looked quite serious when he said, 'How long after you met her before you realized you loved her?'

'I'm not quite sure. It was either a minute or twenty-four hours, and it's going to take me a year or two to find out which one it was.'

'Do you really think, Ted, you can know enough about a girl even in twenty-four hours to know that you love her.'

'Bill, I'm too old to speculate on the chemistry and metaphysics of love. I recognize the point you're trying to make and I know how the people back in London must feel and I know that probably one per cent of their concern is for me as a person. Not being able to be with Sammy could well have been the end for me. There wasn't anything at all to live for. If I'd bled all over the place it wouldn't have helped Sammy; it wouldn't have helped me either. Because of Grazyna I was able to give back to Sammy what wasn't mine to take and still come out feeling happy rather than self-righteous, and with something to look forward to.'

'But, Ted. You've obviously broken up the Berger operation. The boys back in London can finish it all off. You've got a fair amount of dough and a good job to go back to.'

I looked up at Bill. 'Bill, are you married?'

He nodded. 'Yes, I am married as a matter of fact. We've got three kids. We live in Austin, Texas. She's Chinese and we've known one another since she was fourteen and I was twenty and we got married the day she was twenty-one. Her old lady didn't like me so we had to wait, but we knew a hell of a lot about one another before we got hitched.'

173

I sighed. 'Bill, that sounds great and I'm very pleased for you but for everybody it doesn't work out that way. All I can say about Grazyna is that if she isn't right for me then no one is and no one ever will be. It's as simple as that.'

The fingers of Bill's right hand were tapping the table. They looked like Wall's pork sausages, not the small, thin ones but the big family size, and the shrewd piggy little eyes looked across at me.

'You realize she's a fully operational PZPR officer? We've got a file on her at least an inch thick, and although she doesn't operate in the field, we're pretty damn certain that both the CIA and SIS have lost some pretty sharp guys because of her.'

'Look, Bill, the PZPR isn't in the same league as the KGB and every time an officer from the KGB defects, everybody gives three cheers. He's stashed away in that nice little house in Oxford. He gets his pension and a good time is had by all, and half the time you aren't sure he's not playing games with you anyway. So why the big flap about a girl who's a low-ranking officer in the PZPR?'

Bill didn't lift his head but his shrewd eyes looked up from beneath his eyebrows when he said, 'Do you think she'll co-operate, Ted – do you think she'll talk?'

'I've no idea. I haven't asked her and I wouldn't ask her. She may be defecting but she isn't coming over as a defector. She's coming over because we're going to get married. It's as simple as that.'

Bill shook his head slowly. 'No, it's not as simple as that.'

'Well, let's get something else straight first because I think it's the crux of the matter. The CIA were interested in the Berger operation as well as the SIS. The SIS man working on the job – me – flits off to Poland because of pressure about his daughter. Doesn't say a word to anybody about leaving or what he's found out about the operation and I'm damn sure the CIA won't like all that. The SIS won't like it either, and what they won't like even more is that the CIA knows. So how about me? I wouldn't put it past your lot or my lot to let me go to the wall now you know what you want to know. I shan't complain. I'll do my best to get us into West Germany and then we'll head for Ireland.'

Bill used one fat finger to shuffle some crumbs on the table and then he said, 'You're right, Ted, about yourself. Your instincts are fantastic but not where it affects you personally. If you'd used your brain you'd have already worked this lot out. Jim Railton told you there was one reason why you'd been put on this job that he couldn't tell you, and you've never bothered to put two and two together. Your people knew about Sammy about four years ago. It was one of the small bits and pieces that they got from Petrov when he defected in Australia way, way back. It took a long time to get through to London but it was stuck in your file. They took it for granted you'd do anything to protect her so nobody's horrified about that. I've got orders to get you back safe and sound and I've been promised any facilities I want, short of starting another war. I mean what I say, it's the girl who's the problem, not you. So that's what we've got to talk about.'

'As far as I'm concerned there's nothing to talk about. We go home together with your help or we go off on our own.'

Bill looked over at me, sighed and then went on looking.

'You're not going to like what I say, Ted, but it's got to be said. My brief is to get you back and it's also to persuade you not to try and take the girl with you. You know as well as I do that the KGB are hopping mad that you've broken up Berger's operation.' And when he had let that sink in he went on, 'All those R11 devices have already been removed, and if I tell you that twenty-five have already been discovered in computer installations in the U.S.A., you'll realize that they're really after your blood. It's not going to be easy to get you out because this time they'd rather see you dead than alive. The British ambassador has already been told that he and his staff are confined to the Embassy. There are three rings of troops in that area. The frontier police are on full alert and all their leave has been stopped indefinitely, and that applies to the police as well. And we've heard on the grape-vine that your girl friend's old department is working on how to paint the picture so that

175

every Pole in Poland will do his bit to help put you in the bag. Sammy and Yuri have already been sent back to Moscow. This is altogether too big for anyone on their side to lose face. You're not dealing with the Poles now, you're dealing with the Russians. You've got to remember, in the case of the girl, they don't see her as just going off to marry an English spy, they take it for granted she's part of the Berger affair and they're going to teach her a lesson. Even if you get her to Ireland, I wouldn't give you ten cents for her chances of being alive at the end of the year. Take it from me the KGB are going to knock her off just for the hell of it.'

He looked at me to see how I reacted. I realized how undignified I must look. Just a jacket and trousers; no shirt, no tie, no socks, no shoes – no shave.

'Bill, when we did our training they told us that in the long run it didn't pay to bash people about in interrogation. I never really believed that until they started bashing me about. If they'd chatted me up, sooner or later they would have made a point of contact and it would have been only a question of time before I went down the drain, but as soon as the thugs got to work it was me versus them and what you just said to me about the girl was the equivalent of what they did back in Magdeburg and I'm not playing. She'll take her chance with me. Now do we plan for us both or do we shake hands and call it a day?'

Bill had his two hands clasped together, elbows on the table and he was idly picking his teeth with a thumbnail. He seemed to be looking at something about fifteen miles away and it was three or four minutes before he spoke. Then he looked across at me and I was horrified to see that he looked ill. His face was pale and drawn. His eyes looked tired and there were beads of sweat across his forehead.

'Ted, if I level with you I want your promise that you'll listen – try to understand, and that you'll work out something with me no matter what happens.'

I had a terrible premonition of disaster but I had no idea how terrible the disaster would be. 'Tell me, Bill. I won't go off the deep end.'

'Promise?'

'Promise.'

'I had firm orders to bring you back and leave the girl here.'

He was trembling but he said no more.

'But you pretty well told me that, Bill.'

He was shaking as if he were cold and he said it very quietly, 'The girl was to be left here – dead or alive – and if you wouldn't co-operate and insisted on staying or going it alone, I was to finish you both off.'

I found it hurt to move my lips but I could hear my own voice saying, 'My God, Bill, they're terrible people. They all pretend to be gentlemen but they're really bloody savages.'

He stood up, walked over to the fire and kneeled down to get some warmth.

'No, Ted, it's not as easy as that. You didn't take long to bust this lot open but it could have taken months, years even. They've got away with a hell of a lot of secrets. It doesn't look important because it's about industry, money and people. There are no secret weapons, nothing that sounds worth while, but if it had gone on much longer they could have ruined your country and mine commercially. The Depression of the 'thirties would have looked like a bonanza. We'd have had millions of unemployed, no trade and there would have been nothing that anybody could do about it. And they'd have been dusting off some old slogans like "Better Red than Dead" and we'd have had communist governments without a revolution – you just wouldn't have needed one. It was a pretty big prize, and it's got knocked out of their hands and it was mainly you who did it. Your lot picked you because they thought your knowledge of Berger could come in handy. I don't know whether it did or not, but you split him wide open and you can imagine what sort of stink there'd be in the House of Commons and the newspapers if it was found out that they knowingly used a man whose daughter was a Russian citizen and who was known to be emotionally unstable and a sitting duck for any pressure applied to him about his daughter. I wouldn't put it past the KGB to leak this information anyway. It would suit their book and it makes a very good last resort.'

When he finished speaking I said to him, 'Do you think I'm emotionally unstable?'

He smiled. 'I'd have bet all the dough I've got that that would be the point you'd pick on out of all I'd said.'

'Well, do you?'

'Yes, I do. It's why I like you, and apart from that it's what gives you your talent in this game and if I can misquote Oscar Wilde, I'd rather a man had one warm vice than ten cold virtues. If you hadn't got your temperament you could have had a much easier personal life but it wouldn't be so easy to like you.'

'Sounds a bit like an obituary, but I don't see why it affects the girl.'

Bill drew a deep breath. 'Well, I suppose we'd better talk about the girl. I haven't seen an up-to-date picture of her but I have seen a photograph which must have been taken at a wedding or a confirmation because she was dressed all in white and I thought she looked beautiful and she probably looks even more beautiful now but there's something you don't know that I can't tell you about her.'

I could feel my temper blazing and I was annoyed that my voice shook with anger. 'For God's sake, Bill, it's too late for that sort of crap. Don't give me the "She was Stalin's illegitimate daughter" jazz. I don't give a damn if she was, and half the Sunday papers in England would be clamouring for the serial rights of her life story if she was.'

There was almost a touch of anger in Bill Autenowski's eyes. They looked pretty cold when they looked across at me. 'It's not crap, Ted, it's for real. If that girl leaves Poland a lot of people who *might* be going to die will die for certain.' And as he said this the door from the stairs burst open and in came Grazyna. I'd never seen her like this before. She was obviously burning with anger and her face looked altogether different, more grown-up, and not at all soft. When she got to Bill she harangued him, hands on hips like any fishwife. They were talking in Polish and my three words were of no help at all.

The battle went on for over ten minutes and I could see

that he was gradually quietening her down and then in the end she fell silent and, brushing his hand nervously over his crewcut, Autenowski said, 'Well, I'd better give you my congratulations for a start. This is quite a girl you've got here and I think you're a very lucky man. You probably won't believe it but all that lot was to persuade me not to tell you what I've got orders not to tell you anyway, and all of this because she says you've got enough worries already.' He hesitated for a moment and then burst out laughing. 'Do you know what she said? She said "the poor lamb's had enough". Anybody who can say you're a lamb must really love you. But I do understand that you had to leave Sammy behind; you don't know what sort of reception you'll get from your guys in London – and I'm not sure either.'

He looked over at Grazyna and smiled and he got a frosty look for his pains. She had all the air of a girl who was going to stamp her foot at any moment. Still looking at Grazyna he said, 'Grazyna Kujawska, the way you behave make you a grown-up woman and I can assure you that this man is a grown-up man. So because of what you said, I'm going to break my orders and tell him.' And he turned to me. 'Grazyna's been working for MI6 and SIS for two years. She's the corner-stone of a small operation over here. It's not very big, it's not even terribly effective, but for a number of reasons if she goes they'll be able to work out the rest of the network and they'll clobber the lot and that includes Bob Fraser.'

I opened my mouth to speak but he held up both hands. 'No, you just listen to what I'm going to say. I'm going to offer you a deal. If Grazyna and I can work out a way of covering up in the next twenty-four hours, I'll take you both. If we can't do that I go back on my own and I'll leave you two to fend for yourselves.' It was generous thinking but it had a hole in the end of it.

'Thanks, Bill, it's a nice idea but if you two can't make it work out we've lost twenty-four hours and we need them badly. When the chips are on the table there's nothing to stop you from killing us both before you go.'

Bill walked across the room and undid the strap on a

medium-sized suitcase. When he stood up he was holding a hefty automatic pistol fitted with a silencer and it didn't waver as he walked across the room towards me. He was right at the table when he leaned forward and laid it down in front of me with the butt near my hand.

'Will that convince you?'

Even then my suspicious mind made me take it up, ease back the slide and pull out the feed chamber. When I pressed down the top bullet, the spring didn't give. It was fully loaded. Even as I did this he slid a packet of fifty lead-nosed bullets across the table. All we were going to lose was twenty-four hours and I'd already worked out that every day that we could lie low was to our advantage because it would take some of the steam out of their operation. I looked across at Grazyna and she smiled and nodded.

'O.K., Bill, it's a deal.'

CHAPTER TWENTY-NINE

Bill threw some more logs on the fire and Grazyna went into the kitchen to return with hot milk and honey, some cheese and bread. For the other two, most of the tension seemed to have gone because they could concentrate on how to cover up the network and I felt a bit left out of things. Apart from which they were talking in Polish, but Grazyna kept her hand in mine. After about fifteen minutes Bill turned to me and said, 'We've pretty well settled on using Grabowski, but I can't make my mind up from what Grazyna tells me as to whether he'd talk or not if he got caught. We'd need forty-eight to seventy-two hours to sweep the network under the carpet. After that it wouldn't matter.'

'What are you going to use Grabowski for?'

Bill shrugged. 'Nothing much more than taking messages. That part's no problem, it's just how quickly he'd talk if he was caught.'

I thought carefully for a couple of minutes. 'Well, I'd say it all depends on how you sell him the idea. He's been a scavenger all his life. He knows it, but if he didn't know it you can be sure a lot of people have told him. These kind of fellows compensate in their personal lives, mainly with women, and with the women they have a sort of Walter Mitty existence. They talk of big financial deals, international enterprises and that sort of stuff, and the one thing all the stories have in common is that the Grabowski types are heroes and, in my experience, these guys are such convincing liars that they convince themselves. And I would guess that if you could sell Grabowski that if he gets caught and doesn't talk for seven days he's a hero then he'll probably last a couple of days just acting out the part.'

Bill smiled benignly, 'I'll buy that, Ted. That's real good thinking. I know the kind of man you mean and if you tell them they're heroes they'll believe it and they'll play the part till the going gets really rough.'

He turned to Grazyna. 'What do you think, Grazyna? You've seen the guy. Do you think it would work?'

She nodded. 'Yes I do. It's probably the only way and I can't think of an alternative, but I hope he doesn't get caught.'

Bill looked down at his watch. 'It's five o'clock now and I'd better get a message through to Warsaw. We'd have to go through the operator if we used the telephone here and farmers don't ring Warsaw at five in the morning so I'm going to use the transceiver.'

He walked over to the suitcase again and said as he went, 'Grazyna, I want you to send the message. They might just pick it up and they might spot a foreign accent.'

He came back with what looked like a small portable radio set, hardly as big as a cigar box. I leaned over to look at it and Bill said, 'Pick it up.'

I did and it weighed as if it was made of lead. I looked up at him. 'This must be packed full of goodies. What sort of range has it got?'

'Just over four hundred miles on voice and half as much again if you're using Morse.'

He flicked up a small lid on the side and pulled out an almost invisible thread, thinner even than a light fishing line. When he'd uncoiled about forty feet, he took a piece of plasticine and stuck the end of the aerial wire to the ceiling. He touched a small button. In the dim light of the room the aerial glowed red hot.

'What's the heat do, Bill?'

'Well, it's responsible for the long-range facility on the transmitter. I don't know how it does it but I know it's something to do with a thing called F Centres.'

But he wasn't paying much attention to me now. The lid came up hydraulically to reveal what looked like four slide rules. There was a slight smell of ozone and then he was speaking in Polish. Both he and Grazyna were using ear-plug microphones, and it looked as if they'd raised the people at the other end pretty well straight away. After a few minutes which seemed to be a series of check words and passwords, he nodded to Grazyna and she repeated after him sentence after sentence. They must have been on the air for twenty-five minutes and then they took the ear-plugs out. The glow from the wire faded and Bill wound in the filament aerial, took down the bit of plasticine and threw it on the fire.

Graznya and I went to bed and Bill stretched out in an armchair by the fire. It was midday when Grazyna and I went downstairs again. Bill was all smiles. 'Grabowski's agreed to do it. Lapped up the hero bit, and we think the whole network will be clean by midnight tonight. I've been in touch with Frankfurt and they're going to lay on a heli-copter for us. They can only pick us up in daylight and we've got to put some sheets out as markers for them. The helicopter's coming from Vienna. Seems it takes about an hour and a half from take-off to landing. They've got the map reference here and they're working out courses and so on right now.'

'When do they pick us up?'

'Early tomorrow morning. Just after first light, I'd guess.'

'Why the hell don't they come today?'

Bill grinned. 'They've got to work out a diversion, be-cause it seems like the Russians have put up half the War-saw Pact aircraft to patrol the whole of the border area. Okiencie airport at Warsaw has been closed to all traffic, in and out, and it's taking five hours for a train to get across a border because the checks are so thorough. They've closed all roads and there's a general pandemonium going on.'

At six o'clock the farmer came in and switched on his old-fashioned radio and the three of them listened intently, and from the looks they exchanged I could tell it wasn't good news. When it got to something or other about Mao Tse-tung the farmer switched the radio off and Bill went back to his armchair.

Again Grazyna and he talked in Polish for a few minutes till I interrupted and said, 'How about you letting me in on the act.'

'Sorry, Ted. Our bit was the first item on the news and they really played it big. Apparently the Poles expelled

183

forty-two members of the British Embassy staff today, which must mean pretty well everybody except the ambassador himself. All civil flights in and out are cancelled until further notice. The Soviet Union has protested to the British government about espionage activities in one of the Warsaw Pact countries and has cancelled a visit of the Bolshoi, and a concert tour by Rostropovich, and the Chelsea football team is sitting in Moscow waiting for a plane back to London instead of playing Moscow Dynamo tonight. To round it off there's a reward of half a million zloty, a holiday for two at Jelenia Gora, a Warszawa car and petrol for a year for whoever puts you in the bag, government officials included.'

I had a real laugh for the first time in a long while. Bill only smiled. 'Why the big laugh?'

'Oh, just the dough, the holiday for two, the car. You could win more than that every week in one of the *Sunday Mirror* competitions.'

Bill grinned, 'You're just a running dog of the capitalists, Ted. Just be thankful there aren't a thousand Singer sewing machines as runners-up prizes for anyone who's seen a stranger in their district in the last couple of days.'

Grazyna and I went to bed about ten o'clock and it was ten past twelve when Bill burst into the room and shook me awake.

'Ted, I've just been listening to the midnight news. They've got Grabowski. They actually gave his name.'

He was shining the torch on my face.

'How soon can the helicopter pick us up?'

'Not until first light tomorrow – and I mean tomorrow, not today. It's already past midnight. They still haven't worked out a diversion and they don't think they'll get through the air defence without diverting part of it. It seems they definitely can't come in the dark because they can't pinpoint the farm accurately enough on just one run-in without having a beacon of some sort and that would be a dead give-away.'

I looked up at Bill through the glare of the torch. 'Let's get some sleep and we can talk about it at breakfast.'

'O.K., Ted. I guess there's nothing we can do except cross our fingers that Grabowski doesn't talk.'

At breakfast we were pretty well silent. Bill had been on to Frankfurt again but the USAF at Vienna hadn't been able to give a pick-up time although they had worked out a diversion scheme. Grazyna said she'd wander down to the old stone bridge over the river, Czarny having remarked the previous day that there was good fishing to be had there, round the roots of the tree beside the bridge. I said I would join her when I'd had my shave.

About fifteen minutes later when I walked through the farm kitchen there was a stranger talking to the farmer. I nodded to both of them and went out through the door into the courtyard and down the path to the bridge. There were perch, roach and a pike or two in the clear slow-moving stream and I spent an hour pointing them out to Grazyna and telling her how we fished for them in England.

The sun was wonderfully hot and the grassy bank made a beautiful pillow. We lay back and enjoyed the warmth of the sun and I told Grazyna fairy stories about Polish princesses and English knights. Then she reached out for a particularly large buttercup and I watched her roll over on to her stomach, reach out with her long slender arm, and as her fingers touched the buttercup she started trembling violently. I sat up, and standing about ten feet away there was a man in a black leather coat with a black trilby hat. He was the man who'd been talking to the farmer as I'd passed through the kitchen and now he was looking at us.

He was looking at Grazyna more than me and as I watched he stared at me as if he wanted to remember my face, then he turned on his heel and walked over the bridge towards the main road. A few minutes later we heard a car start off and head for Gorlitz.

When I glanced down at Grazyna I saw that she was still trembling. 'The man,' she said, 'the man, is he still there?'

'He's gone,' I told her.

She closed her eyes very tightly and she said in a whisper, 'That was Borowski.'

'Are you sure?'

'Yes, and he recognized me too.'

I reached down and pulled her to her feet.

'We'd better go back and tell Bill.'

I knew that walk back was the last bit of peace we were going to get for a long time. When we passed in under the archway to the courtyard, she stopped and put her arms round me and I stroked the long black hair. She looked like a child and I felt so protective towards her, but she was always wiser than I expected.

As I stroked her hair she said, 'We had our little walk in peace and now you've got to start worrying again.'

Bill was standing with Czarny and as soon as he saw me he said, 'I've got bad news.'

'That makes two of us. What's yours?'

'I've had the tip-off from the embassy that Grabowski started talking two hours after they picked him up and at least two of the network have already been put in the bag. It can only be a matter of time before they come to get us here.'

'Not much time, I'm afraid, Bill. Grazyna and I were sitting down on the bank of the stream and she was recognized by a man named Borowski who's head of the PZPR in Gorlitz. He's a pretty important guy.'

I turned to the farmer. 'He was the man who was in here talking with you this morning.'

'He told me he was from the town hall checking on accommodation and asked whether I was willing to take paying guests. He must have already known you were here.'

I looked at my watch. 'It's nearly two o'clock now. He's had to drive back to Gorlitz. He'll report back to Warsaw, they'll tell him what they want doing and he'll be back here with his men tonight. I don't think they'll try it in daylight because we can see all the entrances to the farm from the bedroom windows and they must know that if we did a bolt they'd probably never find us. They'll probably put a ten-mile cordon round within the next hour but they aren't going to risk flushing us out until they're really ready.'

I turned again to Czarny. 'Whatever happens, you've got some trouble on your hands. It won't make any difference

186

to our situation if you go down to the police station in Gorlitz and tell them that you've got two suspects who pretended to be tourists.'

The Pole smiled and shook his head. 'I think it's a bit late for that.'

Bill said immediately, 'Would you like to come back with us and settle in England or the States?'

'That would be nice. I think it would be best, but I'll have to get a message at the last minute to one of my men because if the cows aren't milked tomorrow morning they'll be in great pain and two are ready to calve.'

'How are the PZPR offices organized?' I asked Grazyna.

'They're all organized on exactly the same basis as the Abwehr.'

'Am I right in thinking they can over-ride the police and the military?'

She nodded. 'Yes, not only over-ride them but can give them orders and use them without reference to Warsaw.'

'How long before Vienna could pick us up, Bill?'

He pursed his lips and shook his head slowly, 'I don't think they're going to be able to do it, Ted. They've been insistent they can't work at night, but I'll see if I can raise them and tell them we're in a spot, but I'm pretty sure they're going to ask us to hold out till early morning.'

I tried to look cheerful. 'Well, we've got one automatic pistol between the four of us and I think we've just got to split up and make our own way because we haven't got any defence if we stick here.'

Czarny held up his hand to be listened to. 'Is it better if we could stay?'

I nodded.

'Well,' he said slowly, 'I can provide the arms, more than enough.'

'Where are they?'

'They're buried in a field.'

'How long?'

'Ten years.'

'We'd never get them in working order. It would take hours to strip them down.'

He gave me an impatient look. 'They won't need stripping down. They'll work first time. You can come with me and I'll show you.' Ten minutes later we were disconnecting the pipe to a water tank that supplied water to the cattle troughs. We drained the tank and together we lifted it off its brick footing. The earth was dry beneath it and the farmer's pointed spade cut the first turf. It took us both twenty minutes of hard digging before the spade jarred and clanged against metal. On the outside was thick tarred canvas then two layers of tarred paper and as we ripped it off there was a beautiful sight. There was a Bren gun with bipod and traverse mounting, two Sten guns, a Thompson sub-machine gun, a Luger pistol, two Smith & Wesson ·38s and four Lee-Enfield rifles, and at least a dozen boxes of ammunition.

I looked up at the Pole. 'How many rounds for the Bren gun?'

'Between four and five hundred, about a hundred each for the Stens and the Tommy and three hundred for the rifles.'

Twenty-five minutes later we were rattling over the cobbles of the courtyard. I gave the Luger and the Tommy gun to Grazyna. 'I'll check the Tommy gun for you, Grazyna. It's a lovely gun, it doesn't have as many stoppages as the Stens. You can just keep firing away with that.'

I looked at the others. 'Have you two ever used a Bren gun?' They both shook their heads. 'O.K., that's mine. Take a rifle each and a Sten gun each and we can keep those guys unhappy for a long, long time.'

At my suggestion each of us checked our arms and the farmhouse kitchen rang to the snapping of springs and breeches, then we all loaded ammunition. Once upon a time I'd been able to assemble a Bren gun in thirty seconds flat and blindfold, but it took me two minutes this time. There was even a spare barrel for the Bren, so even if it overheated I could change over and keep firing. There was some tracer in the Bren ammunition and I kept that out to fire last because I reckoned it would only give our position away until at the end it wouldn't matter. I longed to have just one short burst to try it out but that wasn't on. All the guns were in beautiful condition and nobody had any complaints. Bill had been on to Frankfurt and they obviously thought we were panicking a bit, asked to be kept informed as soon as there was any movement against the farm and implied that if it was broad daylight and there was no enemy aircraft and no wind and nothing more interesting to do, they might lend us a hand from Vienna. They also added a nice touch that the helicopter would be a Sikorski.

The farmer laughed. 'Nice name, nice aircraft, but it will stick out a mile when it comes over the Czech border because, despite the name, we don't use them.'

I did a reconnaisance of the bedroom windows and I set up the Bren gun on a good solid table, setting the traverse locks to cover an arc from the stone bridge up to a big clump of trees further up the stream. I couldn't cover south of the bridge because a corner of the mill roof projected. In the other bedroom I helped Bill and the Pole lay out the ammunition for the rifles and showed them the two most likely fields of fire that I should want covered. I was going to use Grazyna to give my fire orders and carry messages between the two rooms. Suddenly all my depression had gone. It was wonderful to be doing something constructive, not to be just on the run.

I didn't dwell too much on the negative reaction from Frankfurt, and I made Bill get on to them again and tell them about our new armoury. It seemed they were impressed and this is what I'd hoped for. Nobody wants to back a certain loser and that was what we must have looked like before. It's not easy to identify with odd civilians, but once you're talking about Bren guns and Tommy guns it sounds like you're in business – their business.

We had a good meal and it was almost a party. We were all probably avoiding the issues. We each had a bet on what time they'd come, except Grazyna who didn't hold with such levity. The Pole said one o'clock, Bill finally settled for midnight, and just to show them that we needed to be alert, I picked ten o'clock as our hour of glory.

189

CHAPTER THIRTY

They came at seven o'clock that evening. I was sitting on a stool at our bedroom window. I'd just checked the traverse on the Bren for what must have been the hundredth time. Bill had walked in from the next bedroom and was leaning against the wall at the side of the window, smoking a thin cigar. He had just said, 'They won't be here for hours yet and there's some . . .'

The window smashed in and a bullet thunked into the solid wardrobe door. It was fairly low so whoever was firing must be over a thousand yards away. I looked in the mirrors I'd arranged at the side of the windows. The sun had almost set and the elm trees near by threw long shadows like sundials. As the ground fell away to the meadows by the stream, there were swirls of mist and at the stream itself the mist was so heavy that it had closed in completely. The stone bridge wasn't visible. Whoever had fired must have come over the bridge and then taken cover in one of the big clumps of blackberry and elderberry. Because I had been surprised I hadn't heard the shot but it was a single shot so it should be a rifle, but all my instincts told me that it was a smart boy with the lever set at single shots on a machine-gun. Grazyna and the farmer had both come into the room and I waved them down on to the floor.

'If you want to go, Tadeusz, you just go,' Bill said to the farmer. 'You've done enough for us.'

Czarny just said, 'I'll stay.'

I went into the corner bedroom to observe the south bridge, but the great swirls of mist had rolled up to within two hundred yards of the farmhouse. The farmhouse itself must have made a clean and beautiful target as it lay bathed in the late evening sun. There was a blackbird singing in the honeysuckle beneath the window and then there was a burst of five rounds and the windows swung with empty frames and there was plaster and dust falling from a

190

hole where one of the bullets had gone home. This time I'd heard the machine-gun's breech recoiling with that singing, metallic slap, and even without the burst of five rounds I'd have known they were using a Schmeisser. They were out of date when the war ended but they were good enough for us. I could hear the grinding roar of at least two half-tracks down by the stream. They weren't in a hurry because they knew they'd got us but they weren't taking any chances. They were aiming to kill not capture. I moved back into our bedroom with the others and Bill was setting up his transmitter.

He cast a glance at me as I came in. 'I'm going to ask Frankfurt to at least have a go at finding us. It's now an odds-on chance that they won't but at least they can have a go.'

I'd given Grazyna the Luger and I could see she hadn't cocked it and I slid it back and let it snap forward. I tossed up in my mind whether there was any point in giving the game away that we'd got a Bren and I opted for letting them know, even if it only used up ten minutes while they replanned their operation. It could gain us some valuable time. The Bren was lying sideways on its pivot and I set it up so that it was vertical, set the firing lever at automatic, tapped down the handle on the barrel to make sure it was locked in place and gave them a burst of ten over about half the traverse.

This obviously caused some surprise because in the thin evening air there were shouts and counter-shouts, and it sounded as though one of the half-tracks had got stuck in the soft earth by the bank of the stream. Whoever was driving it hadn't got much experience because he'd pulled back the throttle so that the engine was grinding its heart out; I guessed it was digging itself into the soft earth and wouldn't be troubling us that night.

Bill was on net and they were obviously taking notice at the other end. There was about two minutes when he didn't speak and he looked across at me and said, 'I think they're going to risk it. They've got to ask the C.O.' Something must have come up in his ear microphone because he

191

turned back to the set quickly and was uselessly nodding agreement to the operator at the other end. Then he snapped the lid down on the transceiver, wound the small handle at the side which coiled in the aerial and got up off his knees.

'They expect to be here at about ten o'clock but they're not very hopeful that they'll lift us. They say they can pick out the area of the farm but they won't be able to pick out any particular spot. So on seven hunded acres, the chances of them and us being in exactly the same place are pretty remote. They've got a message for you from Joe Steiner.' Bill grinned, 'Joe said "Come home all is forgiven".' And oddly enough that rather weak joke made me feel I was back in the club again.

Someone was shouting at us through a loud-hailer. 'You are surrounded. Come out with your hands up. We will not shoot.'

It stank of inefficiency. I gave them another burst of ten, firing the hosepipe method and they didn't like that.

For the next ten minutes we were under very heavy fire from rifles and an automatic. We could hear clay tiles sliding off the roof and falling into the courtyard, but there was more danger from ricochets than from direct hits. There was a cluster of four shots which went up into the ceiling and our attackers were obviously moving nearer, but they were still too far away and too well hidden by the mist for us to see them. Then I heard a well-remembered thump and a few seconds later the first grenade landed with a loud crack and the cutting whirr of fragmented metal. The first two exploded against the brick wall on the north side of the courtyard. The third and fourth hit somewhere on the big oak gates, and when the fifth landed on the same spot the top of the gates hung into the courtyard and in a grinding, creaking, slow-motion collapse their weight dragged the hinges from the wall and they collapsed on to the cobbles.

The others hadn't had any experience of this kind of game and weren't too happy about it, but what I'd seen pleased me a lot. This operation wasn't under the command of a trained army officer and it looked to me as though the

192

PZPR were giving the operational and firing orders themselves. They ought to have rushed us in the first ten minutes but they were scared.

Then there was the clatter of footsteps on the courtyard and a bunch of five or six people – I guessed it was the farmworkers – went through the archway with a white flag on a pole. They'd almost reached the edge of the mist swirls when they were cut down by machine-gun fire. At least a hundred rounds must have been pumped into them, and any army officer who needed a hundred rounds to kill half a dozen unarmed civilians didn't know his stuff.

I heard Tadeusz Czarny say, 'My God, my God, they didn't need to do that.' I looked at his face. There were tears on his cheeks and I wondered why he thought that the PZPR was softer than its masters in Moscow.

A single half-track came into sight right on the edge of the mist; for a moment the low mist swirled away and I saw the commander and a wireless operator with their heads and shoulders through the turret. I just caught the glint of the commander's binoculars. I lined them up in the sights and screwed the range finder setting back. I estimated that there wasn't any wind because there was very little movement of the mist. They were at about seven hundred yards and I gave them three apiece and as the mist closed round them I heard somebody screaming and the two metallic pings which probably meant I'd been shooting short. I gave another burst of ten into where I estimated the tracks looped over the wheels. There was a lot of shouting going on and it was twenty minutes before they attacked again. This time they were firing one-in-three tracer, and there was nothing to do but to keep our heads down as bullets came looping across to the wall or off the farm buildings and the mill. There were two heavy machine-guns and seven or eight rifles but they obviously weren't certain that we were in the farmhouse itself, and they were trying to cover the whole complex of farm buildings.

There was a lot of damage in both bedrooms but I reckoned that the mill itself was taking the biggest beating. It was a mainly wooden structure and I could see windows and doors hanging down the sides of the walls and they had two grenade throwers trying to knock out the wooden bridge. They obviously suspected that we might use it as a getaway route and it was heartening to see such miscalculation.

I said to the others, 'As soon as this lot stops I want everybody in their places and I want you to fire solid just as much as you can from when I say "Fire" until I tell you to stop. Just cover anywhere you fancy from the clump of elms north of the bridge down to the bridge itself, sights set at about twelve hundred yards and I want one of the two Stens to spray where we saw the half-track.'

I'd hardly finished speaking when the firing stopped. I gave Bill and Tadeusz two minutes to get settled in the other bedroom and I shouted, 'Fire.'

I raked the area where I'd seen the half-track and almost immediately there was a bright yellow glow, then a burst of flame and a few seconds later we heard the explosion as the petrol tank went up. In the light of the flames I could see a dozen or so figures and two more vehicles, a small army truck and what looked like a radio van. Moving the ratchet of the back-sight forward I sent off thirty rounds at the van. We had no binoculars but Grazyna told me I'd made a hit and I shouted to the others to cease fire.

Both bedrooms were heavy with cordite fumes and when I went in to Bill and the farmer I could see that they'd taken quite a beating in there. There was water pouring down from a severed pipe and the ceiling was coming away in one corner. Another ten minutes and it was dark as well as misty. I looked at my watch and was staggered to see that it was only nine o'clock. There were a hundred rounds of tracer for the Bren. The spare barrel and the tracer I gave to Bill and told him to cover with me.

We clattered across the courtyard to the north wall. Over the top of the farm machinery store was a platform which held about a hundred sacks of corn and seed, and when we'd done the tour of the farm I'd noticed two circular windows which gave some light to this grain store. We loaded up the tracer and we fired single rounds in the direc-

194

tion of our friends for the next fifteen minutes. Then we clattered back to the farmhouse again.

For the next twenty minutes there was continuous firing at the north side of the quadrangle and when in the end they started using rockets, large segments of the wall crumbled down and out. In another five minutes the archway itself collapsed with a roar of bricks and rubble and a great cloud of dust hung in the air, and then for nearly twenty minutes there was nothing happening.

We had used up two-thirds of the ammunition and I wasn't prepared to start again. If they got in the courtyard, they'd be sitting ducks and if they didn't, we were safe.

The silence was so complete that we could hear a cow bellowing and the farmer said, 'That's Maryska. What a night to be calving.'

By now there was a slight wind and I heard a clock chime threequarters of the hour. 'How far away is that clock?' I asked Czarny.

He hunched up his shoulders. 'Nearly two miles, something like that,' and then he held up his hand. He was listening. 'Come,' he said, 'let's go down in the courtyard.'

We stood there and he held his head down with his eyes closed and he turned slowly and pointed with his arm to the south-west. 'There's a helicopter coming.'

It was another three minutes before we could hear it and even then I couldn't have said whether it was a helicopter or an ordinary plane. A few minutes later it was there and it flew over the farm buildings and obviously hadn't spotted them. I asked the Pole if he'd got a torch but he hadn't. He asked what I wanted it for. I told him I thought I might be able to make a Morse signal to them, but it was a bit of an outside chance.

He shook his head. 'They'll never see a torch up there.' Then he said, 'You fire at those bastards for five minutes to give me cover and I'll make a signal for the chopper. In five minutes you go to the south wall and come quickly down the farm road and I'll be waiting for you.'

'What are you going to do, Tadeusz?'

He smiled grimly. 'You leave it to me, Englishman. I

195

know what I'm doing.' And he disappeared into the darkness.

I didn't let them use up much ammunition but we took turns in firing continuously for the next five or six minutes. I took the Pole's Sten gun and the rest of his rounds and we clattered down the stairs, through the kitchen and across the courtyard to the south-west corner of the quadrangle. We'd only just arrived there and I was trying to get my bearings when I saw what Czarny had done. The first of the wheat fields was blazing at the corner and the breeze was taking the flames straight down the side of the field. By the time we got there, there were fifty acres in flames. The whole area was lit up and the noise of the burning was frightening. There was a man in some sort of uniform lying spreadeagled at the gate of the field with his hands still clenched round a sub-machine gun. He was dead.

The farmer said, 'They seem to have posted look-outs down all the farm paths.'

He was breathing heavily and one hand was on his chest. The helicopter was about forty feet above the ground, circling slowly, tilted inwards, and the pilot and co-pilot were looking out from the cockpit which was ablaze with light. There was a search-light underneath the belly of the helicopter and after a few preliminary sweeps, its light picked us up. The area we were now standing in was completely burnt out but the ground was very hot and the ashes in the stubble were still sparking and glowing.

The helicopter landed and the co-pilot came down a short ladder and jumped to the ground and ran over to us.

'Which one of you is Autenowski?'

Bill moved forward and said, 'I'm Autenowski,' then he fished in his pocket and brought out an identity card. The flyer looked at the photograph and then looked at Bill and said, 'O.K. How many people have you got?'

'There's one young lady, two other men and myself.'

'Gee, we're going to be overloaded. You'd better get a move on.' He looked at Grazyna. 'O.K., Miss, you get in first.'

196

We were both looking at the helicopter cabin, watching for the signal for the next one to go aboard and I said, 'We'd better let the Pole go next.' Bill nodded and I turned to where the farmer was standing.

I'd seen Czarcy holding his chest and, over the crackling of the burning wheat, I said, 'Are you hurt?'

He just nodded his head and there was something about his face that worried me.

'Never mind, Tadeusz. They'll soon patch you up.'

He shook his head slowly, 'I cannot go.'

'Why not?'

He moved his hand away from his chest. There was a hole, a gaping hole and a great slab of flesh hung down. I could see part of two of his exposed ribs and they were clean, shining white. There was a pink froth behind them, and as he stood the blood welled out of the wound and slowly ran down his chest.

He stood there, no longer a man, just looking at me, imploring me to put it right. The big brown eyes desperately seeking a miracle. No longer a man because he looked like a small child showing a hurt finger to be healed with a Band-Aid.

I looked at his face and I didn't know what to do. I put my two arms round him and cradled his head on my shoulder. I kissed his brow as if he were a small child and said, 'Tadeusz, I love you.' Then I lowered him gently to the ground because he was already dead.

Bill dragged on my arm and we both ran to the helicopter. It's rotors were thrashing round and sparks were swirling as it fanned the burning stubble. I could see Grazyna's face pressed to the cabin window and the pilot was holding the door open. Bill clambered up first but I hadn't got the strength and they hauled me in by my arms.

CHAPTER THIRTY-ONE

The rotors of the helicopter seemed to be clawing desperately at the air. It turned sickeningly, almost on its side, and then we were going up fast. As the lights snapped out the pilot said, 'I'm afraid it's going to be a bumpy ride because we've got to hedge-hop all the way to keep under their radar network.' And for two solid hours he was right. Helicopters may look like dragon-flies from the ground but for us we had two hours of what seemed to be a cross between a bullfight and a rodeo. Then suddenly the lights were on and the co-pilot turned in his seat. 'Well, you don't look too bad, all of you. We can take it easy now. We're over the border and we were able to fix up a NATO night-scheme. They're patrolling the border so they won't skip over after us.'

About fifteen minutes later, he leaned the helicopter on one side and pointed down. 'That's Vienna,' and so it was. You could almost hear the music. We landed in a small military bay at Vienna airport, and as we walked across the apron, the pilot said, 'I'll take you to where you've got to go but then I've got to peel off and get back to Linz.'

Inside the main airport buildings he took us down a corridor and showed us to a door marked 'Flughafen Wien-Polizei Hauptquartier'.

'Just knock and go in,' he said.

We did that, and inside was an amiable-looking civilian who came round from the other side of his desk and said, 'Good evening. Which one of you is Autenowski?'

Bill identified himself and introduced the rest of us.

'Well, now, I've been asked to look after you all and put you on the next plane to London. That means you've got just over an hour with us here. I've made arrangements so that you can have baths, shaves, a meal, whatever you want.'

Bill looked across at me. 'I think I'd better get on the

198

blower to London, Ted. Maybe I can smooth down a few ruffled feathers. How about you and Grazyna go off and tidy yourselves up and have a meal and I'll join you for coffee.' As Grazyna and I were going out of the door, Bill said in a low voice, 'Don't forget you're both security risks and the risk starts when you get down the corridor. Would you like a gun?'

I grinned. 'No, thanks. I've got one. I kept Grazyna's Luger.' Bill shook his head in disbelief and shuffled me out after Grazyna.

My cleaning up took ten minutes; Grazyna's twenty, but she looked beautiful and fresh as an apple, and she linked her arm in mine and we walked down to the restaurant. As I pushed open the doors the loudspeakers were giving out a lovely, lush version of 'Drunt' in der Lobau' and before we found a table I whisked her on to the small dance floor and waltzed her round and sang the words in her ear.

We had Wiener Schnitzel and 'Kaffee mit' and when we got to the second round of coffee, Bill joined us. He said, 'Jim and Joe had fixed to meet you at Heathrow but that's been called off. You two are booked in at the Hilton for tonight and they'd like you to hang on there till they come round in the morning.'

It was two in the morning when the BAC-111 took off and Bill was very specific about where we should all sit, with Grazyna next to the window, with me next to her and Bill on the seat in the aisle. The seats in front of us and behind us had been removed and I was glad to see they were taking no chances. We ordered a celebratory bottle of champagne from the hostess and when she was giving Bill his change he said, 'Will you tell me, Miss, about fifteen minutes before we're due in at Gatwick.'

She smiled her pretty, superior smile, 'I'm sorry, sir, but we don't go to Gatwick. This flight's for Heathrow and I'll let you know when it's fifteen minutes before our ETA.'

Bill nodded and then settled down with what appeared to be a textbook on tropical fish. An hour and a half later, the intercom crackled and an old school-tie voice said, 'This is your captain speaking. Owing to poor visibility at London

Airport, Heathrow, this flight is being diverted to Gatwick. Transport to the BEA terminal at Kensington is already waiting for you. We shall be landing in about fifteen minutes.' Bill looked across at me and winked. The next time the hostess came down the aisle she cut Bill dead.

Gatwick has never been one of my favourite landing spots. It has all the air of a servants' entrance. When we reached immigration there was one of our chaps there and the three of us were waved through.

The security man said. 'There's a message for you in our office.'

The message was for Bill to phone London, and when he came back out of the inner office he said, 'I've just been talking to Joe Steiner. As you probably guessed, we re-routed that aircraft to Gatwick as a precaution because the KGB are running round London like wet hens. We don't think they know what to do but we didn't want to put any ideas into their heads, so if you're not too tired they'd like you to go straight up to Whitehall from here.'

I turned to Grazyna. 'How about you, sweetie?'

'I'm fine.'

'O.K., Bill.'

'There's a car outside for us.'

And there certainly was. It was an almost brand new Jensen. As we came over Westminster Bridge the light was still on in the tower at the House of Commons and I wondered what they were discussing that was so urgent that they'd all had to be called back from their buckets and spades. The driver swept off the road on to Horse Guards' Parade and we were the only car there and lights were burning in two or three of the War Office windows.

I called out to Bill, 'I won't be two minutes. I'm just going to walk Grazyna over to the edge of the park.' And right by the war memorial I gave her a kiss and holding her face in both my hands I said, 'In case the men don't think of such a thing let me say it – welcome to England.' She laughed, remembering what she had said to me in Warsaw. She kissed me again and then, looking over the corner of St James's Park at the silhouette of some building round about Queen Anne's gate, she said, 'Look, that looks just like the Kremlin,' and she was dead right, it did.

When we got to the doors of the War Office Joe Steiner was there and he was actually wearing a suit, and Joe not being properly English, we had hugs all round. The cypher offices were working but nobody else as far as I could see and we clattered our way up to the first floor where we were shown to a very palatial office. There was Jim Railton, a junior whom I'd never seen before and lots of empty coffee cups. Jim Railton was very nice to Grazyna and then we were all invited to sit down.

Jim looked over at me. 'Before I start, I've got a couple of things for you here; a passport for yourself.' He handed it over to me. 'And a passport for Miss Kujawska.' He gave her a warm avuncular smile as he handed hers to Grazyna, adding, 'You'll get a new one of course when you change your name.' Then he threw a small box to me which I only just caught. I opened it to find a beautiful diamond engagement ring with a small note which said, 'With love from the tax-payers'. When I hesitated he said, 'Go on, for heaven's sake, put it on for her.' I did. If she was pleased why on earth did she cry?

Ever tactful, Jim Railton said, 'We thought we'd better have a council of war because you two are going to be sitting ducks for the KGB unless we do something about it. Joe and I haven't had time to discuss this so we might as well put our heads together. The reason we interrupted a good night's sleep was that we thought that whatever we're going to do we'd better do it quickly to stop any little games they might be planning.'

I asked him, 'How much of this has got out to the Press?'

He pursed his lips. 'Nothing at all. Yesterday one of their chaps in London asked for political asylum, so we took the opportunity of declaring a hundred of their staff in London "persona non grata". We've got quite a few bargaining points there and it's kept the Press well occupied. It's caused a bit of a furore. The House was recalled today at the request of the Leader of the Opposition who deplored what he called "this unfriendly action towards the Soviet

Union". What he doesn't know yet is that a couple of his hangers-on will be going inside tomorrow, or, I should say, today.'

Then Grazyna said, 'I feel the person we should be worrying about is Sammy. What can we do to protect her?'

Jim Railton picked a non-existent thread from his trouser leg. 'We know she's quite safe right now and we can bring some quite genuine diplomatic pressure to bear because she's still a Ward of the English High Court and she has British citizenship. We can let them know we shall be keeping our ears open about what's happening to Sammy.'

Grazyna shook her head. 'That won't be enough. If the KGB want to put pressure on Edward or me they wouldn't worry about diplomatic ritual.'

Joe Steiner interrupted. 'Jim – everybody – why don't you just leave this whole circus to me. I can get them off everybody's back in ten minutes.'

He was standing hands in pockets as if he was bored with the whole proceedings, letting the children have their say before dad took over.

Jim Railton said, 'What have you got in mind, Joe?'

He grinned. 'Now that's a trade secret, Jim. All I need is one little telephone call to Moscow. I'll have a quick chat with Yuri and he and I'll do a deal.'

'What sort of a deal?'

'I've told you, I'm not telling. It's a trade secret. All I'm saying is that it will work and it won't cost a cent. I know what you guys will come up with. Some half-baked threat that if anything happens to Sammy or Grazyna or Ted we'll knock off one or two of their people. It won't work. I've been through all that caper before. All sorts of people get knocked off and everybody gets so goddamn bored that in the end they lose count of whose turn it is. Meantime nobody's benefited but the undertakers. Why don't you just leave it to me?'

'O.K., Joe, there's the phone.'

Joe turned round and sat himself at the desk. 'Which one is it?'

'The green one.'

202

He lifted the phone. 'Get me Yuri Andropov in Moscow, person to person, no secretaries or under-strappers. Tell him who's calling – Joe Steiner, London.'

He put back the earpiece and used a very ornate letter opener to titivate his nails. He was obviously quite sure of what he was going to do and quite sure it was going to work. He wasn't even giving thought to it because he turned to me and said, 'There's some mail for you, Ted, when we've finished. Where are you going from here?' But before I could answer the green phone rang.

'Hello there, Yuri. What's the weather like in Moscow tonight – now, now, Yuri. You know it's a good old English custom to ask about the weather before we get down to the horse-dealing – sure we are. What's that? – yeah, I quite agree, the PZPR could do with a hell of a lot of re-organization but don't fret. They're new boys – they've got to learn the ropes. – Yeah, I said don't fret – it means don't worry – sure I know you're worried. Now, let's get down to the facts. Bailey and the girl are here in London – oh, for God's sake, we're not treating her as a defector – I thought you Russians were romantic – it's just Romeo and Juliet stuff. No, of course we're not telling the Press – why the hell should we do that? – the what? – chucking out the diplomats, oh that's a different story. Sure, Yuri, we reckoned you'd throw some of our guys out but after all we haven't got a quarter in our Moscow embassy compared with your place in Kensington. Anyway, that's for the diplomats to sort out – you and I are just plain, honest soldiers. By the way, forgetting business for a few minutes, how's that beautiful blonde wife of yours – what's that? – no, not Olga, I thought her name was Maryka – Yuri you must forgive me – we had her down in the records as your wife – I could've sworn your room at Claridges was for Mr and Mrs – sure pal – sure – I understand. Yeah, it's like what we have in the Royal Navy here. We've got a special toast – yes, a toast – what you say before you all drink together – that's it. Well in the Navy they say "to sweethearts and wives, may they never meet". No, of course, it won't be mentioned to a soul, Yuri, it'll never go out of these four walls, believe me. No it isn't just Bailey and the girl. It's a question of young Sammy, Bailey's daughter. You know she's a Ward of the English High Court and a British citizen and if your boys started chasing her around, we would really have to start to raise some hell – sure we'll do a deal – O.K. what is it you want to know – will we what? – speak up Yuri, there's no need to be shy. I see, you wanna know if we'll vote with the Americans in the Security Council for the proposed Israeli frontier revisions.'

Joe looked appealingly at Jim Railton who gave him the thumbs down. 'O.K., Yuri, if I give you the answer to that we've got a deal, eh? – O.K. We won't be voting with the Americans – sure it's possible our boys could change their minds but I'd consider it part of the deal to keep you fully informed at every stage. That's agreed then, Yuri, so over here you call your dogs off Bailey and the girl and you're responsible for Sammy in Moscow or wherever she goes. Fine, fine – let me know when I can do something for you – Dosvedhanya.'

He hung up and with his chin in his hand he looked round at us all.

'Everybody satisfied?'

And I said, 'Joe, you're wonderful.'

'I know,' he said, 'I'm great.'